Pamela D. Holloway cannot remember a time when she didn't write. It started at school with essays, turning into short stories.

Married to her childhood sweetheart at 20; the next years were filled with babies, who, as they grew older, listened to her magical stories of imaginary lands and weird animals.

Now free to turn to novels, she has written a number of books and has finally been encouraged to look for publication. This is her second published book. Her first being *A Different Kind of Life*, available on Amazon.

Dedication

With love and thanks to my husband.

Pamela D. Holloway

CLAIRE'S STORY

AUSTIN MACAULEY PUBLISHERS™

LONDON • CAMBRIDGE • NEW YORK • SHARJAH

A CIP catalogue record for this title is available from the British Library.

ISBN 9781788482844 (Paperback)
ISBN 9781788482851 (Hardback)
ISBN 9781788482868 (E-Book)

www.austinmacauley.com

First Published (2018)
Austin Macauley Publishers Ltd™
25 Canada Square
Canary Wharf
London
E14 5LQ

Acknowledgements

Janice Barnes, who somehow managed to read my scrawl.
My sincere thanks to the Production Team at Austin Macauley
for all the help and support I have received.

Chapter 1

As the plane began to taxi along the runway, Claire looked out of the window, at the receding buildings. Her sister, she imagined, would be walking resolutely towards the car park, her fair shoulder length hair moving with each step, her soft camel coat open at the front, revealing a long, slim body, clothed in a cashmere sweater of pastel cream and trousers, almost exactly the same shade as her coat. *She would*, thought Claire, *have that irritatingly happy expression on her face that seemed to be part of her these days. All very well for her*, Claire's thoughts ran on. Fiona had left home, running away; when she was sixteen, she landed on her feet: two husbands, two children and famous!

The plane started to climb at quite an alarming angle. For a moment, Claire felt fearful; it was, after all, the first time she had flown. Everyone around her seemed calm enough, apart from Lenny, his book forgotten, his knuckles clenched and white, looking into some distant unseen horizon.

Unusually for Claire, she empathised with her son. She supposed he must feel rather strange too. They had left Edinburgh hurriedly (rather as Fiona had done all those years earlier). Now, she was heading for a new life, but she was lumbered with a 10-year-old.

Mr Lennard had moved in with her mother, when she was five years old. She had been encouraged to call him Uncle Len. After her mother's death, Claire, now 18, had married him. It all seemed so exciting, so grown up, taking her mother's place. Now she had to get away.

Fiona had been surprisingly supportive. Their contact had been very limited for years. Len had forbidden her to mention her sister and when Lenny had asked if he had an aunt, he had been told brusquely 'no' by his father. But he did, he did. It was thoughts of Aunt Fiona that were helping him not to be frightened now. He had pretended when they met in the Charing Cross Hotel two days ago that he didn't want to meet her. He felt his face redden as he remembered how rude he had been.

"I don't have an Aunt Fiona," he had said when she introduced herself and bent over him to give her a hug. He had stiffened, and she had drawn back, but not before he had felt the softness of her and smelt something so beautiful that seemed to be part of her. His mother wasn't like that; she was hard and spiky, like her red hair, and he always thought her perfumes smelt like air freshener. He glanced sideways to find her looking at him. Their eyes met and held.

"You alright?" she asked.

"Of course," he answered, determined not to show he was scared.

Lenny wasn't actually scared of the flying. It was everything that had happened in the past few days. The rows were nothing new. His parents always rowed, but this time he was shocked to see his father hit his mother then watch his father leave the house, his mother had said that they were leaving. They were going to Canada to visit her old school friend, Ellie. They had to pack quickly, just one case, and quite a small one at that.

Lenny had looked around his bedroom, the one that Uncle Stewie had before he left to join the Army. He wondered if he would miss it, but thought that going to Canada sounded rather a good adventure. He thought he might miss his father, but not all that much. Neither of his parents talked to him much, and he had rather become a solitary boy, enjoying his books and computer games, which he played hour on hour in his bedroom.

Yes, thought Lenny as he surveyed his bedroom for the last time. *I shall miss my computer games, that's all.* School and school friends were of no particular interest. He did what he had to do to keep his teachers happy; he spent most of his lunch breaks in the library or computer room and had few friends and even those, only at a casual level. He looked at his mother again; she was still looking out of the window. He noticed that she was clutching her handbag very tightly.

He'd seen the slim envelope that Aunt Fiona had handed over along with the flight tickets and heard her say as she did, "That will keep you going for a little while."

His mother had gasped and then said, "Two thousand, Fiona; that's very kind."

His aunt had smiled, "What are sisters for, Claire?" He had watched as they clung briefly together.

This time, sadly, Aunt Fiona had not attempted to hug him; instead, she had handed him a parcel and held out her hand. Solemnly, he shook it, and then as if on impulse, she had bent down again and hugged her nephew. This time he hadn't stiffened. He had let himself be held against her for a brief and blissful moment. Now he closed his eyes and thought about her, and wished that she was his mother.

Chapter 2

The flight to Vancouver was a long one. It gave Lenny plenty of time to look at the books Aunt Fiona had given him. The one he liked best was called *Canada, a Land of Contrasts*. It showed pictures of cities, snow-covered land and snow-filled woods. It showed harbours, full of yachts. It showed ports and prairies. It showed horses running free and others being ridden. It showed pictures of bears catching salmon as they swam up stream in the icy waters. What a place they were going to. Claire's mind was full of excitement too. Ellie's Christmas card every year always said, 'When are you coming to visit us?' So she knew she would be welcome.

Ellie had married a dentist; and judging by the occasional exchange of address, they had moved steadily up market. Their home was on Vancouver Island and Claire envisaged something like the Isle of Wight, which she had visited once with Len and Lenny in their early married days when Lenny was a baby. She had no idea how she would get to Vancouver Island, but with Fiona's traveller's cheques in her bag, she knew she and Lenny could book into a hotel in Vancouver for a night or two whilst she made enquiries. Something prompted her not to telephone Ellie in advance. They would just arrive!

"Have you enjoyed your flight with Air Canada?" the prettiest of the stewardesses asked Lenny.

"Yes, thank you," he answered politely. In fact, he had thought it a bit boring after the first excitement.

"Wish all our young passengers were as well behaved as your son!" He heard her say to his mother.

"Oh, thank you." His mother sounded surprised and, he noted, quite pleased. He breathed a sigh of relief; it was not always easy to please Claire. He always thought of her as Claire, but he always remembered to call her Mother. He had only made the mistake of calling her Claire once; he could still remember. He had come running out of school on his first day, so pleased to see her waiting for him at the gate.

"Claire, Claire," he had called.

"Don't you ever dare call me that again, Lenny," she had said, squeezing his arm so tightly that it hurt. "Just remember, I am your mother." From that day on, he called her Mother, though, before that he had, like most small children, called her Mummy. She was not Mummy anymore, a voice had said in his head. She is my mother.

Claire followed the crowds; everyone else seemed to know where to go. Passport control asked whether she was on holiday or business. "Holiday," she replied airily, knowing she had no intention of leaving. If Ellie could find a rich husband, so could she. The suitcase arrived after a few moments, and they followed the exit signs. It was late evening in Vancouver and when they went through the doors, a cold blast of air hit them as no Edinburgh air had ever done.

"Put your coat on, Lenny," she said as she snuggled into the pure cashmere coat Fiona had insisted on buying her before they left England. Lenny put on the duffle coat Aunt Fiona had given him and put his hands in his pockets to keep them warm. There was something in one of the pockets and pulling it out he found a pair of warm gloves.

"Look, Mother," he began. But Claire's attention was focussed on getting a taxi and getting out of the wind and rain. It all looked so bleak, she thought; perhaps Canada wasn't such a good idea after all.

Once in the taxi, her spirits revived. Cold was no problem when you have the right clothes, at least she had the money to buy some, but she would have to be careful – buy enough to look well off, but not to use up too much of the two thousand pounds.

The taxi driver, as good as his word, drove them to a hotel in a nice central part of town. The shops were bright and exciting looking, and Claire felt her spirits lift. "This is an adventure," she kept repeating to herself like a mantra.

Once inside the hotel, they quickly checked in. "Yes, of course, we'll share a room," she replied somewhat sharply. "I'm sorry," she added, seeing the girl's expression change, and she didn't want to begin life in Canada by alienating people. "We are very tired; we've been travelling for a long time."

The pleasant young woman smiled sympathetically. "Please don't worry, we've a lovely room for you and your son and room service is 24 hours so you don't have to go to the restaurant if you don't want to. Though, that's open 24 hours too."

Claire picked up the door card, declined help with the case and headed for the lift. A weary Lenny followed on, hoping that soon, very soon, he would be able to lie down. He fell asleep over a supper tray and Claire picked him up and laid him on one of the two large beds. She undressed him and put his pyjamas on without him seeming to realise. Suddenly, she felt a tenderness she had not felt before. He was ten, but he looked little and fragile. He was a good kid, really, he hadn't been any bother. She bent down and kissed him on the forehead, something she hadn't done for years. To her surprise, the kiss seemed to have half pulled him out of sleep; his arms came up and round her neck. "Goodnight, Aunt Fiona." Claire stiffened and unwrapped his arms, feeling, for the second time in the past few days, entirely jealous of her sister. She pulled the covers roughly over the sleeping boy and turned her attention to the wine bottle that needed finishing off.

Chapter 3

The next morning, Lenny was awake before his mother. He noticed the empty wine bottle and knew, with any luck, he would have a while to himself before she woke. He dressed as silently as possible in the bathroom, and then opened the curtains a little to look at the city. It had been dark, and he had been too tired to bother about it the night before.

He wondered what the time was; his mother had mentioned a time difference, but he had no idea whether it was backwards or forwards from home.

Lenny sat for quite a long time, watching from the fourth floor window. Traffic streamed in a constant flow, little figures bundled up again, the weather walked briskly like streams of ants.

Claire groaned; she had always hated waking up. Now her head was full of doubts about the wisdom of her journey; she felt alone, and was alone, apart from Lenny who didn't really count. Claire was alone for the first time in her life. 'I'm thirty-four,' she said to herself. 'I'm grown up,' but inwardly, she acknowledged that she wished that there was someone more adult to 'look after her' as there had been all her life.

"Breakfast," she announced. Lenny turned reluctantly from the window and then suddenly realised he was very hungry. "Ring room service, Lenny. I want coffee, orange juice and croissant. You tell them what you want."

As he hesitated by the phone, she snapped her fingers impatiently. "For heaven's sake, Lenny, the number's on the phone. I think its nine." And on that note, she got out of bed and went to the bathroom.

Feeling decidedly apprehensive, he picked up the telephone and listened to the silence. Looking carefully, he saw the list of numbers. Operator, housekeeper, concierge, room service. His mother had been correct; it was nine.

He pressed the digit somewhat fearfully. Within seconds, a cheerful female voice said, "Room service, what would you like to order?"

Lenny took a deep breath and repeated what his mother had said.

"Anything else?"

"Yes," he said, feeling braver by the minute.

"I'd like orange juice and bacon and eggs, and oh yes, toast and marmalade," he added as an afterthought.

"Room number, Sir?"

"I don't know," said the boy miserably as Claire walked back into the room.

"For heaven's sake, child, what don't you know?"

"The room number," he responded a shade defensively, thinking Claire should have told him.

"Silly boy," she said, taking the telephone from him and, at the same time, pointing out the number which was written above the list he had looked at so attentively minutes before.

How was he supposed to know that 4214 was their room?

Claire put the telephone down and seeing his face beginning to pucker, felt a pang of remorse. Just because she felt jaded, she didn't have to take it out on him.

"It's okay," she said, patting him lightly on the shoulder. "It's all a bit strange, isn't it?"

He wasn't accustomed to her being nice, and it made it even harder to blink back the threatening tears, but somehow he did. He knew she couldn't stand him crying.

Breakfast arrived shortly after, and the waiter turned the trolley with their breakfast on into a table by putting up the side leaves. It all looked and smelt appetising, and as soon as the waiter had left, they both sat down on the chairs he had placed for them and began their first Canadian breakfast.

There was a small jug with what looked like golden syrup, only darker.

"What's this, Mother?" Lenny wanted to know.

The waiter had put it by the side of the plate with his bacon and eggs.

Claire smelt it. "Maple syrup," she answered, her mouth full of deliciously hot croissant.

"What's it for?"

"I suppose it's to put over your bacon."

Lenny was bemused. "How funny," he said, putting the tiniest portion on the side of his plate.

But almost instantly, he was back for more. "Um, it's brilliant."

He sounded so pleased with himself that it made Claire smile. Perhaps, he wasn't such a bad little boy, after all.

"Lenny", she began seriously. "There is something we have to discuss."

He hated it when his mother used that tone. It was invariably something unpleasant.

Claire wanted to get this over quickly. "When we get to my friend Ellie, we are going to pretend that your father is dead."

"But he isn't," blurted Lenny, looking at her strangely. "You said we were just leaving him. He's not dead, he's not, he's not."

Claire sighed; this was going to be as difficult as she had imagined.

"He is as good as dead to us," she said. "We've left him, and our life in Scotland over, and I'm going to find you a new and better daddy here."

"But you're married to father." He knew something was wrong, surely, people got divorced if they were going to marry someone else. Quite a lot of the class had stepmothers and stepfathers, but he felt sure they were divorced.

"We've left the country," Claire said smoothly. "I can marry anyone I want to now, but it's more convenient if they think he is dead. Do you understand, Lenny, you must not let me down?"

Her voice had a hard edge to it and he knew that there would be no further discussion, he must get used to the idea.

After a few moments of silence, Claire told him they were going shopping and going to get tickets to Vancouver Island. She had no idea how to get there and would have to check at the desk before they went out.

An hour or so later, they were once again at the front desk.

"We need to get to Vancouver Island this evening or tomorrow," Claire informed the clerk. "How do we get there, and can you arrange it from here?"

"Of course, Madam," was the response.

It seemed there was a choice between flying and a ferry. Claire had had enough of planes, a ferry would be easier and Lenny could go off and explore, and leave her in peace. The clerk informed her he would book the ferry tickets and would have them for her by the end of the day. Claire agreed the cost could go on her room bill. Then she and Lenny went through the big glass door and onto the street.

Despite their coats, they both shivered. Lenny put on his new navy blue gloves.

"Where did those come from?" Claire asked sharply.

"I found them in the pocket. Aunt Fiona must have put them there, or the shop, I suppose," he added as an afterthought.

"You're lucky. She didn't buy me any!"

A few yards down the street they came to one of the big stores the doorman had told them about. Thankfully, they went inside, glad to be out of the cold and the lightly falling snow.

Claire had lain in bed, making lists in her head. She didn't want to buy too much and spend too much of the precious money, but she had to buy enough to look as if she was quite well off.

"We'll do your shopping first," she said, pushing Lenny ahead of her into the lift.

Lenny didn't usually like shopping, but this store was big and bright. All the Christmas decorations were reminding him that although it was only October, Christmas was not too far off.

Claire bought him ankle boots, warm socks, two pairs of trousers, several shirts and sweaters, and a fleecy jacket that he could wear as an alternative to his new coat. She then took him to the toy department and handed him over to an assistant who said she would gladly keep an eye on him whilst his mother shopped for clothes for herself. Lenny could hardly believe his luck. It was a paradise of computer games and electronic gadgets beyond his imagination, and toys in such abundance that he felt he could stay there for a week and not get bored. The assistant smiled indulgently, pointed out her counter area and told him to keep coming back so that she could be sure he was all right and enjoying his visit. For the first time in his life, Lenny found himself talking to some children of his own age quite easily. They were so friendly, so different from the boys he had known back home.

Meanwhile, Claire was having almost as much fun. A smart, black wool dress for either day or evening, depending on what she put with it. A grey suit with a red blouse. It was almost Christmas! Some smart knee-length boots. She never wore boots, liking to show off her long slim legs, which she felt made up for the rest of her, all bust and no waist. She had vowed that when she had some real money, she'd have her boobs cut down to size; meanwhile, she tended to wear her things very tight, not realising it emphasised rather than diminished her 'problem'.

She had noticed how Fiona's less flamboyant boobs had caused heads to turn. Perhaps, once back at the hotel, she would go and have a bit of a makeover. She patted her spiky red hair. She didn't want to go back to 'mousey', and she liked wearing lots of makeup; the idea of a makeover was put on hold.

Lenny was unaware of his mother watching him; he was totally absorbed in a computer game. Claire felt a pang of guilt. He was obviously so happy. She wished she actually felt more than tolerant and sometimes less than tolerant affection for him. She had wanted a baby; she had felt somehow it would make her feel 'grown up' and important. She had thought if she had a little person to fuss over, she would feel more contented.

When he was born, she had looked at the diminutive creature handed to her by the midwife and felt nothing, nothing at all. She couldn't bring herself to breastfeed despite the encouragement of the nurses and as for changing a soiled nappy, she had felt repulsed. Her inadequacies and unwillingness to cuddle or coo over her son were noted, of course, but put down to the hormonal changes that had taken place at his birth. The staff would have been more concerned had they realised that things never changed. Claire never neglected her son, but she never loved him either. His father either spoilt him or ignored him, so his first ten years had not been particularly happy, though knowing no difference, he accepted it as the norm.

Now, looking at him, Claire felt a pang of guilt. She had taken him away from all the familiar things. For the first time, she realised that he was totally dependent on her. She felt inadequate and not a little afraid.

Please God, she found herself thinking, *let everything work out all right with Ellie.*

As if sensing eyes on him, Lenny looked away from the screen and met his mother's eyes. For a few seconds, their eyes held. Lenny sensed something that he couldn't articulate; it was as if his mother was seeing him for the first time.

Then her expression changed again, the familiar look returned. "Come on, Lenny," her voice, a shade of impatience, was almost comforting in its familiarity. With reluctance, he took his hands off the keyboard and with one last look at the screen, moved towards her.

They made their way to the travel department and bought a larger suitcase with a pull handle and four wheels, which Lenny thought was very smart and was happy to pull along as they went outside to hail a taxi for the short journey back to the hotel.

The desk clerk spotted them coming in, weighed down as they were with shopping bags and a suitcase. "Mrs Lennard," she called.

Claire told Lenny to wait where he was and headed over to the clerk. For one dreadful moment, she thought perhaps Len had tracked her down but the clerk was smiling and holding out some tickets.

"The ferry, Mrs Lennard; your tickets, 6 o'clock today, is that alright for you?"

Claire breathed a sigh of relief. The ferry tickets, she was on her way to Vancouver Island and Ellie, the last part of the journey, was only a few hours away.

She smiled gratefully at the clerk as she took the tickets.

"How long do I need to get to the ferry?" she enquired.

Between them they worked out what time Claire should leave the hotel, and Claire left it with the clerk to organise a taxi to take them to the ferry port.

"Well, that's all organised, Lenny," she said as she got back to her son, waving the tickets as she spoke. "We leave at 5, so we'll have some lunch, then pack."

Lunch was a great success. Lenny loved the choices on the menu and Claire, ever aware of her figure, enjoyed a Waldorf salad and several glasses of red wine. Lenny ate a banana split for dessert whilst Claire looked enviously on, wishing she could have one as well.

Packing was easy. The small case they had arrived with fitted easily into the bigger one. She packed their new purchases around and on top of the smaller case.

At 5 o'clock, they left the hotel, both of them excited for entirely different reasons. For Lenny, it was the end of the journey and a new home with mother's friend. He didn't quite understand and hadn't liked to ask how long they would live there, and when they would have their own home again, but he did wonder.

Claire was thinking about Ellie. The last time they had seen each other was when they were both 13. They had been friends at primary school and then their friendship continued when they found they were in the same class at secondary. Claire remembered that Ellie had been so excited the day she came to school and announced to the entire class that she, her brother and parents were going to live in Canada. Lots of excitement followed the announcement, and their teacher took it as a good opportunity to ask her class to do some research and write a report on life in Canada from trappers to city dwellers. It was only Claire that was silent. Ellie was her best friend; they shared their secrets and their plans for rich husbands and big houses and servants. They both knew these were dreams; they would both have to work. Ellie had also set her heart on university, but Claire was no scholar and the thought of further study after school seemed unnecessarily boring.

Ellie had been as good as her word and had written regularly to Claire for the first two to three years.

Then the letters became further and further apart, partly because Claire seldom bothered to answer them – but for years, she did write a long letter to her friend at Christmas and over the years their contact had finally become the exchange of Christmas cards with the latest news either on a sheet of paper enclosed with the card or just a few scribbled lines. Ellie's messages always finished with, 'And when are you coming to visit?'

Now, as the taxi sped along the road, the first doubts crept into Claire's mind. What if Ellie didn't want her to stay? Perhaps, just perhaps, it was just one of those things people put on Christmas cards and are then horrified when people announce a visit.

Perhaps, she thought, she should have telephoned Ellie from the hotel. But no, they had made a pact years before that they would be 'forever friends' and that nothing and nobody would change that. Claire sat back in the seat, feeling more relaxed. All would be all right.

Chapter 4

Lenny found the ferry fascinating. Claire, who had bought herself a magazine, settled herself comfortably in the lounge.

"You can you go and explore," she told him. "But don't get lost, don't bother anyone and come back in half an hour."

"Yes, Mother," he replied, glancing at his watch.

If his mother said half an hour, he knew she meant it!

"What an obedient boy." A man spoke from the depths of a nearby chair. "I wonder if my son would have grown up like that."

Claire was intrigued. "Don't you have your son living with you anymore then?" she asked, suddenly feeling guilty about Lenny's father.

"In a manner of speaking," the man paused and a shadow passed over his face. "He died, you see."

Claire was shocked. She knew she wasn't motherly in the accepted sense, and she often wished she didn't have to drag a small boy everywhere with her, but if he died, she imagined she would feel sad. The silence between them was uncomfortable, but the man seemed to pull himself together.

"My name's Hugo," he added his surname but she didn't quite catch it.

"Claire," she said, holding out her hand to meet his.

They chatted easily after that, with no further mention of his dead child. He wanted to know where she was going on the land, and she told him to visit an old school friend. Lenny came back for the third time.

"Only half hour more," Hugo said, glancing at his watch. "Can I give you a lift? My car is at the ferry port."

"Thank you, no," replied Claire.

"Fine," replied Hugo, assuming she probably had her friend lined up to meet her.

Lenny came back for the last time. Claire handed him his coat and put hers on. With her new fur hat and cashmere coat, she looked quite elegant. Hugo had had a jolt of surprise when she had pulled off her hat earlier and revealed her red spiky hair but had soon forgotten that as they chatted.

"I'm sure we shall bump into each other again," he said, holding out his hand. "There are only about 250,000 of us on the island."

Claire smiled.

"Then I'm sure we'll meet again," she said.

They both laughed.

Hugo patted Lenny on the back.

"Have a great time, young Lenny, won't you?" Lenny nodded.

There was a judder as the ferry came to a halt; people milled this way and that.

In moments, Hugo had been swallowed up in the crowd.

Claire held back, she didn't want him to see her hunting for a taxi. She hadn't wanted to accept the proffered lift as she had no idea where Ellie lived. *Hugo*, she mused.

For a moment, she wondered if this could have been Ellie's Hugo but it was just too much of a coincidence.

By the time they were back on terra firma, most of the passengers were scurrying for their cars or getting into the taxis that had come to meet the ferry. The rain was miserable, but it was milder, more like autumn back home.

A taxi drew up, and the driver put her case in the trunk – not the 'boot', she noted – she handed him a piece of paper on to which she had copied Ellie's address from her address book.

"Take about ¾ of an hour," the driver told them cheerfully, holding open the door for Claire and her son. "Visiting, huh?"

"Yes," replied Claire quite abruptly, not caring to be drawn into a conversation with him.

He took the hint and apart from an odd word or two spoken to Lenny, there was silence in the car.

Claire's hard intake of breath as the car turned into the drive did not go unnoticed by the driver.

"This is one of the best houses in the area," he said.

Claire made no reply.

The house was lit up like a Christmas tree, with lights in every window. It was an impressive place by any standards. The sweeping drive led to a central island where a fountain played, lit from somewhere below. Then she saw a magnificent double-doored front door with white pillars on either side.

"Is this Ellie's house, Mother?"

"Of course, it is," snapped Claire, suddenly feeling a shade nervous.

Perhaps, she should have written or at least telephoned in advance. Well, it was too late to worry now; they were here and that was that. She paid the driver, who drove off into the night leaving mother and son alone in front of the door.

Claire took a deep breath and rang the bell. As she did so, she turned to Lenny.

"Two things, Lenny; remember, your father is dead and for God's sake, behave."

"Yes, Mother."

All the excitement of going on the ferry and meeting the nice man evaporated; he suddenly felt homesick for his bedroom, his computer, even the familiarity of his school. He hated his mother for dragging him so far away from home. Though he didn't like his father, he felt uncomfortable that he had to pretend that his father was dead.

The doors opened and a woman of around fifty, with her hair neatly drawn back from her face and wearing a simple navy-white collared wool dress with long sleeves, smiled at them.

Momentarily, Claire was thrown. Had they come to the wrong address? Had Ellie moved?

"Who is it, Nancy?" Claire heard a voice calling from within the house.

"Claire Lennard. She will know me better perhaps as Claire McInnes and my son, Lenny."

The voice within called again. Nancy turned and repeated what Claire had said. There was a pause then.

"Let them in, Nancy, at once, out of the wet."

Claire and Lenny walked into what looked like a film set to both of them. A huge curving staircase, on which about halfway down stood a glamorous looking blonde, hair pulled high on her head and wearing a strapless evening dress of cascading black chiffon, shot with diamante trimmings.

The hall was vast. A beautiful glittering chandelier hung over a centrally placed round table. Everywhere she looked, Claire saw beautiful pieces of furniture or objects, d'art on top of a mantelpiece set over a blazing hearth, or in glass cabinets of which there were a number.

Lenny watched, fascinated, as the beautiful lady walked down the rest of the stairs.

"Claire?" she said as she drew closer, incredulity in her voice. "Claire McInnes, I don't believe it."

Lenny watched as his mother and this angel, although she was in black, she was, thought the boy, how he had always imagined angels to look.

"I hope you don't mind," Claire began feeling somewhat out of her depth amid all the opulence.

"Mind, why should I? I'm delighted!"

It was strange seeing Claire again after all these years. Their lives were literally miles away from each other. She even wondered if she had sent a card last Christmas. In all the confusion, she probably didn't.

"You look amazing, Ellie. Stunning, in fact."

"So do you, Claire, so do you!"

But she couldn't help thinking that with her spiky red hair and the tightest of tight clothes and all her makeup, her friend looked a bit like a high-class tart!

She mentally rapped herself over her knuckles for being so uncharitable.

A man appeared at the top of the stairs struggling with his bow tie.

"Ellie, come here, I can never do the damn thing and you've deserted me."

"Hugo, come down, my dear school friend – you've heard me talk about her – has just arrived."

As he came down the stairs, Hugo saw it was none other than the Claire he had met on the ferry.

Claire realised at exactly the same moment, and they both burst out laughing.

Ellie looked mystified.

"What is it?" she asked. "What's so funny?"

They both tried to tell her at once. Ellie looked at the small boy, his eyes now heavy with tiredness.

"We met him", he pointed, "on the boat."

"Right," Ellie spoke brusquely. "Nancy, we have to leave now for the ball, we are already late."

She glanced half accusingly at her husband.

"Please, put Lenny in the nanny's room and Mrs Lennard in the room on the other side, not the adjoining one," she added hastily.

Nancy nodded. "Of course, Mrs Howard."

"And supper for Lenny and a meal for Mrs Lennard!"

Nancy nodded again.

"Claire, I'm so sorry, but it's the yacht club charity ball tonight. We are already running late. We'll catch up in the morning; my housekeeper will look after you." She picked up a fur coat that was lying casually on one of the button-backed sofas and looked questioningly at Hugo.

Reading the unasked question, he said, "I left my coat in the car."

They were gone.

Wow, Claire thought inwardly, her mind spinning with thoughts of her, very sophisticated friend, Hugo, the house, the housekeeper.

"You must be tired, Mrs Lennard. I'll show you and your son to your rooms and bring something upstairs for you both. That will suit you better than coming down, I think." Claire nodded her affirmation; she was longing to have a look around, but there was plenty of time for that in the morning.

"Should I call you Nancy?" She wasn't used to staff.

"As you wish," was the smooth response.

Lenny's room was pleasant. Bed, comfy chair, fireplace, bookshelves fitted to the wall, filled with books.

"The bathroom," Nancy opened a door leading from the bedroom.

"Your own bathroom, Lenny, aren't you the lucky one?"

Lenny sat down on the bed, overwhelmed and tired.

The housekeeper saw the black circles under his eyes.

"You get him to bed, Mrs Lennard. I'll just show you your room and bring up a supper tray for him straight away!"

Claire's room was next door, a bit further along the corridor. It was a lovely big room with a king-sized double bed and also a door off, which the housekeeper opened to show that she too had her own en suite.

Lenny was as she had left him, stuck sitting on the side of the bed. She felt a sudden sympathy for him. All this must be a bit strange – God it was strange enough for her.

By the time Nancy reappeared with a tray, on which stood a glass of milk, a banana and a hastily put together ham sandwich, Lenny was already asleep.

"I'll leave the tray," Nancy said in a kindly voice, "in case he wakes up hungry in the night!"

"Thank you! Shall I come and collect anything?"

The housekeeper looked slightly taken aback. "Mrs Lennard, if you just unpack your things and perhaps run a bath if you like, I'll have a light meal made for you in half an hour."

"Not too light," Claire laughed, feeling suddenly surprisingly hungry. Relief, perhaps, at having arrived at her destination at last.

It was Ellie who woke her the next morning, full of concerns about how she had slept, apologised for having to leave in such a rush the previous evening and wondering how long she could stay and whether her husband would be joining them.

Claire, never at her best in the morning, tried frantically to gather her thoughts and make the right responses. "Yes" she had slept like the proverbial log in the beautiful bedroom; they would, if they may, stay for a week or two whilst she looked for somewhere to live.

If Ellie was taken aback, she appeared delighted – "You are planning to live here; here on the island?" Claire nodded.

"But your husband, can he just give up whatever it is he does, just like that?"

"Len is dead," Claire said, speaking in what she hoped was an impressively solemn tone of voice.

"Oh, you poor darling. Whatever happened?"

Claire thought quickly. Why hadn't she planned that she might be asked this very question, Lenny too?

"It was an accident," she said. "Lenny doesn't know the details, I would rather you didn't discuss it with him."

Ellie put her hand over Claire's. "Of course," she said sympathetically. "I will tell Hugo not to mention it either."

Mention of Hugo reminded Claire of something Hugo had said on the ferry. His son had died.

"Ellie, your little boy. I didn't know. I'm so very sorry."

Claire felt genuinely sad for her friend. She remembered the baby pictures Ellie had sent and little bits of information as he grew.

"How old was he?"

"Six. Look, Claire, I really can't talk about it too much, some other time. It was so horrible. He just died in his sleep. Oedema of the throat, they said. One in a million chances."

A sob broke from her.

"You see, I can't talk about it."

It was Claire's turn to put a hand out and squeeze that of her friend's.

"Poor Ellie, but you'll have other children."

"I can't," Ellie said flatly. "I can't, Claire, and that's that."

She pulled herself together and stood up. "Half an hour, Claire Lennard; that's all the time you have until breakfast. See you in the dining room."

And she was gone, closing the door gently behind her.

Claire showered and dressed, then woke Lenny before she went back to their room to put on her face and do her hair.

Damn, she wouldn't have time to put on the gel. She brushed her hair and it lay smoothly against her head. Actually, she thought it didn't look too bad. It was also a long time since she had seen it like that!

Lenny was not in his room when she went back to collect him, so she walked down the magnificent staircase which reminded her of the one in *The Prince and the Show Girl*, the old Marilyn Monroe movie with Laurence Olivier.

Following the sound of voices, she crossed the hall and found the dining room, which turned out to be the breakfast room the housekeeper told her later when she was being shown around the house.

Lenny and Ellie were deep in conversation. The little boy, now recovered from the journey and looking brighter than she had seen him for a long while, was listening intently to what Ellie was saying.

"Hello, am I late?"

For a moment, Claire felt like an intruder.

"Claire, come and sit here," Ellie pointed to an empty chair at the round bible. "Hugo has already left, I'm afraid. He has his first appointment at 9 am."

The housekeeper hovered by Claire's right elbow. "Porridge, bacon and eggs, sausages. What can I get you?"

Claire would have loved porridge, but Ellie's elegantly slim figure made her feel more than ever that she must watch hers.

"Just black coffee and toast," she responded as she spread her napkin on her knee. Lenny was silent, he knew better than to chat with his mother in the mornings. If he did, she would generally scream at him to 'shut up'. If Ellie noticed the change, she made no mention of it. It was only weeks later, when she and Hugo were talking about the 'situation', that they both commented on Claire's apparent unconcern for her son and Lenny's changed demeanour in her presence.

Chapter 5

The next few weeks sped by for Claire. Hugo and Ellie had a great social circle, and she was soon being included in social events. On a number of occasions, she was invited out by one or another of their bachelor, widowed or divorced friends, but to date, it tended to be one or two dates at most. Either because she found out that they weren't wealthy, or they realised that she was only interested in money. 'A gold digger' was one of the more usual and less colourful epithets describing her. 'A tart' was one of the unkinder ones.

In fairness to Claire, thought Ellie, *she does look better these days*. Her make-up was considerably less than it had been at first and with both Ellie and Hugo saying how much they liked her hair now that she had continued to wear it smooth. The spikes were a thing of the past.

Lenny seemed to be changing. He had been invited to meet a number of boys and girls of his own age and once the initial reserve was gone, he was making 'real' friends for the first time in his life.

The weather had turned much milder, and it was now early December. Hugo had taken Lenny to the yacht on several occasions and having made sure he was keen to try sailing, had taken him out for several short sails, wearing both a life jacket and safety harness.

"Don't want to have to dive in and get you out of this icy water, old chap," had been Hugo's way of getting Lenny to agree that what he had at first said was namby-pamby.

On one occasion, Claire had gone with Hugo. Ellie was playing bridge, Lenny was out with friends and Hugo asked

Claire if she would like to see the yacht. Claire had no idea what to expect. The boat looked much smaller than she had imagined.

"It's 40 feet," said Hugo defensively. "Two heads."

"Two what?" Claire laughed.

"Toilets, land lubber."

"Why heads, no, don't tell me, I don't think I want to know!" She was however impressed when she saw 'downstairs'. The master cabin at the back of the boat had a double bed that one could walk around. The fore cabin had a double berth that had to be scrambled up into. A tiny galley, a central table and curved sofas on either side.

"It's like a caravan on water," she said.

Hugo was insulted.

Claire had the grace to realise that she had gone too far.

"I'm sorry," she said. "I want to look around again."

They stood side by side in the main cabin. Suddenly and unexpectedly, he put his arms around her. Claire turned towards him and let him kiss her. Her mind was clear. She had to think. If he made love to her, which he obviously wanted to, would he leave Ellie for her? If it was just a one-off, what did she gain except, perhaps, power over him? She didn't like sex, she never had, really. The boys at school had been amateurish and Len had been, well, clumsy and old. She had married him for all the wrong reasons. Whilst her mind raced, she let him kiss her. He started to open her blouse and she let him lower her on to the bed before she reacted. "No, Hugo, no. This is all wrong," she managed to sound indignant without seeming cross.

"But, Claire, I need you. Since Robert died, Ellie won't let me near her. She's cold now. I can't get close to her anymore." Claire bit her lip in exasperation at her friend. Silly woman, she would lose him. She was seriously tempted, a plan was formulating in her mind.

"I can't stay at the house, Hugo, if we…"

"I'll get you a flat," he said, his voice muffled as he kissed the breasts he had released from their imprisonment.

"What breasts," he groaned as he sank into their depths and then sucked at her firm nipples.

"You promise, Hugo, a flat?"

32

"Yes, yes," he said, now moving his hand downwards to tear at her trousers. She wriggled from underneath him and undid the trousers, pulled off her knickers and pulled off her sweater and bra. Standing there in total nakedness, he couldn't help but compare her voluptuousness with Ellie's spare form with its tiny breasts. He pulled off his trousers and threw himself on her, where she now lay waiting for him.

Fortunately, as far as Claire was concerned, it was all over quite quickly. She responded automatically, feigning an orgasm that she didn't have and listening to his groans with a detached mind. He would get her a flat. This was the down-payment.

"Thank you, thank you, darling Claire." Claire came back to the moment.

"I better have a shower," she said matter of factly. Hugo sat in the salon, his head in his hands. What had he done? He had never been unfaithful to Ellie. He loved Ellie. His mind spun as thoughts chased one another like clouds across an angry sky.

Claire came back from her ablutions and sat down on the opposite side of the salon, the table between them.

"I'm sorry," Hugo began.

"I can't stay at the house, you do realise, don't you?"

"Of course, I'll find a flat, straightaway. I can come and see you there."

What was he saying, he didn't want her and he wanted his dear sweet Ellie, not this...this tart! But, God, her breasts, he could feel himself getting hard again, just thinking about her.

As if reading his mind, Claire said, "Hugo, pull yourself together, we have to leave soon. If you look like this, Ellie will know."

"You stay down here, Claire, in the warm. I'm just going to take her out for a quick sail."

Claire shrugged and settled back into the comfort of the sofa. She drifted in and out of sleep, the motion of the boat lulling her, rocking her, and at times when the boat seemed to lean fiercely one way or another, either nearly rolling off the sofa or being thrust into its depths. Finally, everything was silent.

Hugo put his head through the hatch. "We're back, Claire. Time to wake up."

"If you think I have been sleeping with all that clacking and banging!" Claire began.

Hugo grinned, "You did. I popped down once or twice."

"Take me home," said Claire. "I've had enough of the sea for one day."

That night Hugo told Ellie that he had slept with another woman. He couldn't live with himself unless he 'confessed', yet he knew that Ellie might reject him forever if he told her the truth. He didn't mention Claire and Ellie didn't ask who. She listened to him as he begged her forgiveness. There were tears in both their eyes. "I've missed you so much, Ellie. I've been grieving for Robert too."

"He was my son," Ellie said, the tears falling unbidden.

"He was my son as well," Hugo's voice broke the sobs.

They were sitting either side of the fireplace in their bedroom. Ellie suddenly held out her arms.

Hugo moved swiftly and knelt on the floor and put his head on her lap.

"I love you, Ellie, only you. I've been a fool."

"So have I," she said brokenly.

That night, for the first time for a year, they lay in each other's arms. There was no lovemaking, but there was a peace between them and the beginnings of a new life.

Next morning, Claire looked cautiously from Ellie to Hugo. Hugo wouldn't meet her eyes. Ellie looked different. She had dark circles under her eyes, but despite this she looked happier. Hugo came around the table and kissed her upturned face. A look passed between them of complete understanding. Claire was bemused and confused. Lenny asked permission to leave the table. He had arranged to meet some of his new friends. They were going fishing and Lenny had been promised a 'go' with a spare rod that one of them promised to bring along.

"Wrap up warmly, Lenny," Ellie said, blowing him a kiss.

Lenny grinned in response, and Claire felt quite left out. *It's almost as if Ellie was his mother*, she thought.

"Claire," Ellie began, her tone unusually serious.

This is it, thought Claire, waiting for something terrible to be said that would change their friendship forever.

"Hugo tells me you want to leave, to find a flat and get a job."

Claire's eyebrows shot up. That was news to her, but clever Hugo to come up with that scenario.

"We were wondering if you would like to leave Lenny here with us."

She held up her hand as Claire started to speak.

"Look, Claire, I'm going to be completely honest with you. Since Robert died, I think a part of me died with him. I didn't want Hugo near me. I almost felt as if I hated him. In some way, I blamed him.

"Well, last night he told me something that upset me, hurt me terribly, but in some curious way, it brought me to my senses. I don't want to lose him to someone else, and I could, Claire, I really could.

"Anyway, we talked quite a lot about a lot of different options. One was to adopt. Then I, we, talked about Lenny. He seems to have started to come out of himself. I'm sure his father's death must have been such a terrible experience for a small boy. He could stay here with us, indefinitely, if you would be prepared to let him. In the few weeks you've been here, he is already making friends. He could start school straight after Christmas."

She paused.

"I'm sorry I'm not giving you a chance to get a word in edgeways." She laughed slightly nervously.

To say that Claire was flabbergasted was an understatement. To have her own flat, paid for by Hugo. To leave Lenny here, which, she had to admit, would suit her very well. *What bliss*. He was happy here; he was happier than he had ever seen him. Why not leave him here?

Ellie glanced at her nervously. "I'm sorry, Claire, if I've upset you with our idea. I quite understand you probably need him near you. After all, you're grieving too. How thoughtless I've been."

Claire had to stop herself laughing out loud.

Instead, choosing her words carefully and managing to sound convincingly sad, she said, "Dear Ellie, how kind, how thoughtful of you and Hugo. Actually, Lenny is happy here. You're right. He seems to have shaken off the death of his father since he's been here. I think it's a wonderful idea, but of course," she added, quite cleverly, she thought, "Lenny will have to be consulted."

"Oh, Claire, of course, of course. How wonderful, and you'd come and see him every weekend, wouldn't you?"

Claire wasn't so sure, but she nodded as if in agreement.

That night, when Hugo arrived home, he had made an effort to be early after Ellie had telephoned and told him the idea of Lenny staying with them had Claire's blessing. He managed to rearrange two of his afternoon appointments, giving him time to speak to rental agencies who said they had several flats of modest size for rental. He arranged to see them the following day. Now he wanted to be home to see Ellie and make sure Claire had said nothing, though, from what she had said on the telephone, Claire was being very agreeable.

Lenny was surprised that after dinner his mother did not tell him to go straight up to his bath.

Instead, they moved from the dining room to the library with its big leather chairs, smell of books and of burning logs. Lenny loved this room; it seemed slightly mysterious to him. He had never seen so many books, not even in the school library in Scotland.

The three adults looked solemn. Lenny was worried. What had he done wrong? His boots, that's what it was. They were soaking and Claire had told him they were ruined. No, it couldn't be that; why would Ellie and Hugo be there?

"Lenny, we have some news for you," began Ellie.

"Are you happy here?" Hugo asked.

Lenny looked puzzled.

Of course, he was happy. He had never been so happy before. What news? Had they found out that his father was still alive? He looked anxiously at Claire.

"Oh, for heaven's sake," Claire sounded impatient. "Just tell him. They want you to stay with them here, Lenny. While I go and get a job and live in a small flat. You wouldn't like that at all, would you?"

"Claire!" Ellie exploded. "That's not the right way at all. Lenny," she said gently, "Hugo and I would love you to live with us for as long as you want. Your mummy will visit all the time, and you can visit her too. There is a lovely school, and you already have friends. Would you like to come and live with us?"

Lenny looked from Hugo to Ellie and back again. Was he hearing right? Would he like to stay here? Of course, he would! His beaming smile said it all.

Ellie held open her arms and Lenny went into them as if that was where he belonged. Hugo sitting on the arm of the chair, ruffled his hair and then three pairs of eyes looked anxiously at Claire.

For a moment, Claire felt jealous. Jealous at their obvious delight in each other. Then she felt a freedom she had never felt before. She was free. Hugo would find her a flat. She would have to work, but not too hard, just enough to keep her in clothes and a bit of food, and Lenny, well, he was obviously delighted with the plan.

"Good," she said finally.

That word sent a shiver of pleasure through the three people watching her so closely; they each interpreted it in their own way.

Good, thought Lenny, *it means it's good to be rid of me.*

Good, thought Ellie, *it means she feels her son will be safe with us.*

Good, thought Hugo, *it means she will keep her counsel, not tell Ellie about yesterday.*

"It will be a new beginning for all of us!" Hugo summed up all their feelings.

Chapter 6

Within a few days, Claire was ensconced in the flat Hugo had found. He had worried that she might not like it. He needn't have been concerned. The door opened directly into the main room, which had views over a busy street but with the triple glazing high enough up for the noise of traffic to be not even a distant sound.

One quite large bedroom and one smaller one.

"More like a storage room really," Hugo apologised-.

An adequate – if small – kitchen, with a breakfast bar and a bathroom with a separate free-standing shower corner.

Claire tried not to appear too excited, but she was thrilled.

"Claire," Hugo began diffidently. "I'm sorry. I owe you an apology about yesterday. It should never have happened. I promise you it won't happen again."

Claire put on a concerned expression. "I understand," she said, managing to put a slight break in her voice.

"You are sweet, Claire."

"But the flat, Hugo. I don't know if I can afford the costs, you haven't told me what they are."

"I've paid the first six months; it was the least I could do; we'll see how you are placed then. Is that alright?"

Alright? It was brilliant.

"Thank you, Hugo. It's most kind of you."

God, she thought, *I should have been an actress; he has no idea how I feel!*

They went back to the house where Claire packed her things, said goodbye to them all and went off in the prepaid taxi that had been ordered for her.

She might have been surprised if she had been a fly on the wall. Ellie and Hugo encircled Lenny and hugged him to them.

"If you feel homesick for your mummy, you must tell us," said Ellie. "We are kind of your adopted family, Lenny," said Hugo, feeling a happiness that, unawares, this small boy was already giving them.

He was coming out of his shell more every day. The morose little boy that had refused to acknowledge his aunt in London seemed to be someone else. He felt really happy except for one thing.

"If I'm sort of adopted," he began. "Can I have your name? I hate being called Lenny Lennard, it sounds so stupid."

"You would rather be Lenny Howard?" Ellie said softly.

He nodded.

"What do you think, Hugo?"

"I think we have to ask your mother first. But if she is agreeable then I don't see why not."

"And I could go to school with my new name?"

They smiled at each other and at him. "Of course," they chorused, "why not?"

And so began Lenny's new life.

Claire stepped into the lift, suitcase in hand. She was so excited. She felt like a kid again, no perhaps not, being a kid had not been much fun. She grimaced and banished thoughts of her childhood from her mind. She let herself in, opened the case and ran around in delight. A few colourful cushions on the white sofa. A pot plant here or there. She had never had any interest in being a homemaker, but she felt a sense of pride in her own, very own home. Even if it was paid for by Hugo. She smiled: it had been so easy and he felt guilty!

The first few days were blissful. She lay in bed late, she went out and had breakfast, then wandered from store to store. She bought one or two items of clothing, but realised despite the flat being paid for, her money was slipping away. She would have to find work. Apart from anything else, she still wanted plastic surgery. Her breasts were half as big again as she wanted them, and although she knew that men liked them, they didn't have to carry them around!

She would get a job, she resolved, and start saving for surgery!

It was somewhat depressing to look at the job ads but one finally caught her eye. Under bar staff. The Vancouver Island Restaurant is looking for a trainee to become assistant to the wine waiter. Neat appearance, good educational background. Good with people. Hours 11:30 – 3:30 and 7:30 – 11:30. Good pay for the right person. Claire loved the sound of the hours. She could lie in bed every morning. It couldn't be too arduous a job. She rang the number to make an appointment for an interview.

"Bring your CV," she was told.

She had no CV. She wasn't phased; she would concoct something that would satisfy them.

Claire decided to wear the black woollen dress with the long sleeve. Her hair without the gel was now smooth to her head. She had to admit that it did look a bit classier. She had been to the hairdresser so now she had a light fringe and the rest of her hair now hung just below her ears in a neat bob. She had also been trying to cut down on her makeup a bit; both Fiona and Ellie had inspired her with their looks and though she would not want to be as dull as either of them, she recognised that she had perhaps been a bit over the top.

She stepped back from the mirror. The dress was tight over her bust, but it was well cut and her figure looked good. Her lipstick was bright red, but she had subdued her eye make-up a little and reduced the blusher on her cheeks. She put on the cashmere coat and her fur hat. Not bad at all, she decided, turning this way and that, seeing herself from all angles.

Unbeknownst to Claire, Michael Brown had only had one applicant for the trainee post. Most people reckoned that the hours in a restaurant seldom turned out as advertised and the pay was as a general rule, poor. This, despite the fact the Vancouver Island Restaurant was one of the smartest restaurants in the city.

Claire's appointment was 9:30 in the morning and she arrived outside the restaurant at least ten minutes too soon. She had asked directions and realised she could walk but it had taken her half the time she had anticipated. Just about to wander off and look at local shops, she cast a glance at the façade again. She had to admit it looked quietly expensive. Her glance caught the eyes of someone inside the restaurant who smiled at her. She smiled back and decided as she had been seen she might just as well go in.

Michael had noticed the young woman and wondered if she could be his prospective employee.

"One shouldn't", he told himself, "judge by appearances, but in her obviously expensive coat and fur hat she looked more like a customer than a prospective employee."

It was disappointing; with only one applicant he had been hoping she might at least be the right one. He opened the door.

"Claire Lennard?" he enquired.

She nodded, slipping off her coat as she spoke. She couldn't get used to the intensity of the heat inside the buildings. He couldn't help a mental 'phew' – what a figure, long slim legs and a pair of bosoms, although lightly encased, shouted out their very obviousness. He caught her glance and laughed. He felt momentary discomfort.

"They are enormous, aren't they? As soon as I can afford it, I shall have them cut to size."

He winced noticeably at the thought.

"Please come through," he said, bringing the necessary formality back into the proceedings.

She followed him into a pleasantly furnished office and sat on the chair he indicated.

"Well, Claire," he began. "Tell me about yourself."

"I'm recently widowed," she began, putting on a suitably sad expression. *Appeal to the emotions first*, she thought.

"I decided to carve a new life for myself in a new country and Canada had always interested me and plus, I have a dear friend and her husband who live on Vancouver Island, which is why I came here."

He nodded sympathetically and with interest.

She has spunk, he thought, *to have taken such a big step after such an obvious trauma.*

He had seen the way her bottom lip trembled as she spoke of her recent bereavement.

"Claire, do you have any experience of bar work at all?"

She thought for a moment and decided if she lied she would soon be found out. "My husband provided for me, he never wanted me to work, so no, to answer your question, I have no experience, but I am a quick learner."

"Right," he smiled at her keenness. "A quick test."

She frowned. "A test?" she queried.

"Nothing to worry about if you are good at mental arithmetic." Claire breathed a sigh of relief.

She was good at mental arithmetic because it had become a way of life for her to squeeze extra money out of Len. This had been when she was a child and he was still 'Uncle Len'. Thoughts of her childhood flashed through her mind. Fiona leaving home so precipitously when she was 16. Mummy dying. Len and her sleeping together and marrying – and the birth of Lenny.

But before that, when she had been sent to do the shopping, she had soon learned that Len never looked at the till receipts. For some extraordinary reason he trusted her. She learned how to keep back a portion of the change every week and if he asked the price of anything, she would always tell him a few pennies more, never too much, she had been clever.

"Yes," she replied. "I think I am good at mental arithmetic."

Michael had watched her expression with interest; her face was fascinating. In the few seconds that she had taken to respond to his question, a myriad of expressions had crossed her face.

He found himself wondering about this young English woman. She was probably considerably deeper than she first appeared.

"Right," he said. "Bar work, which is where you start, can be hectic in the extreme. So, we will imagine you have an order for the following."

He handed her a price list as he spoke. "Here are the prices." He glanced at the list, wines, spirits, cocktails, beers.

"I'm ready," she smiled. "A double whisky, a glass of wine, a cocktail and three German beers and one Canadian beer. Got that?" She nodded, not speaking in case she forgot something.

Thank goodness, she had done lots of shopping and the dollar and cents held no mysteries for her – she quickly calculated and gave him the total.

His smile told her she was correct.

"Well done, Claire. I'm impressed with your speed, but you do realise that sometimes the pressure in the bar can be a lot more pressurised than this."

"Of course," she said, her heart beating fast. She hadn't wanted to work, but she found, perhaps for the first time ever, she was really interested. She wanted the job.

"I normally ask for references, of course," Michael said smoothly. "I imagine your friends, Mr and Mrs?"

"Howard," Claire completed his sentence.

"They will be happy to give a reference."

"Right, then come and meet Harris."

Harris was the bartender; he was a slight man, about 40, with thinning hair and oozing energy. He almost bounced down the bar to meet her.

"Hi."

His voice was surprisingly deep for such a slight figure.

"Hi," Claire returned his smile and held out her hand to shake his outstretched one.

"Your new bar assistant, Harris."

"You mean I've got the job?" She sounded so pleased Michael knew he had made the right decision, even without checking the references.

Harris looked pleased too. She would go down well behind the bar with her lovely, full figure. Even he could appreciate that and he would enjoy telling Peter about her tonight.

"I want to show you the restaurant now, Claire," Michael spoke, interrupting the beginning of an animated conversation.

"This is where – if all goes well – you will eventually be working as assistant wine waiter."

Claire had almost forgotten the restaurant. The bar seemed pretty good to her.

They walked up the stairs to the first floor restaurant. It was quietly and expensively furnished. Big windows overlooked the harbour; the tables were set with white damask tablecloths and silver cutlery and condiments gleamed as did the crystal glasses. A beautiful chandelier hung from the centre of the room and smaller chandeliers hung at intervals from the ceiling. Small posies of fresh flowers, each as perfect as the next, made a centrepiece on each table.

"It's stunning," Claire said, totally impressed.

"I think so," Michael said, pleased with her reaction to his pride and joy.

"When can you start, Claire?"

"Tomorrow?" Claire even surprised herself at her keenness.

Michael looked even more pleased.

"That is excellent. Let's go to my office, and we can discuss salary and clothes."

"Clothes?" said Claire questioningly.

"Of course," Michael replied. "Very important, I believe."

Claire was fascinated. Was she to be dictated about her clothes? She had a moment of doubt. Perhaps, she had been too eager to accept the job.

Once back in the office, Michael talked first about her salary.

It didn't sound all that much to Claire, but as he explained, she would make considerably more if she treated the customers with the proper attitude.

"You will find", he said, "that they frequently say 'have one yourself.' Never, under any circumstance, have anything other than mineral water or a soft drink. There is no drinking on duty. Is that understood?"

Claire nodded.

"However, the money they give for 'your drink', you can put into your tip section of the till and you will find it accumulates quite quickly.

"Now, clothes," Michael continued with barely a pause. "The dress you have on today is perfect, do you have others similar?" Claire shook her head, suddenly aware that her wardrobe of tight, skimpy clothes would not suit Michael at all.

"Right," Michael continued with barely a pause. "You will have a small clothes allowance. Your first month will be trial, perhaps for both of us." He smiled, softening the words as he spoke.

"So, I will give you enough to buy one other dress. Once the month is over, I will, every six months, give you a small dress allowance so that you can increase your wardrobe. However, bear in mind that if you are promoted, as I hope you will be, to assistant wine waiter, you will be expected to wear a black suit and white blouse, but that will be at least 12 months down the line." Claire's head was buzzing, a job, a dress allowance, Michael Brown, Harris, something or other.

What a morning.

She glanced surreptitiously at her watch. It was 11 o'clock. She had been here an hour and a half.

Where had the time gone?

"Right," Michael stood up. "Tomorrow, 11 o'clock on the dot."

He held out his hand, "Goodbye, Claire Lennard. I look forward to having you as a member of Vancouver Island restaurant staff."

"Thank you. I look forward to working here."

That afternoon, she rang Ellie and told her about her new job. "It's a lovely restaurant, Claire. So many of our friends use it. It's terribly expensive, of course, but worth every penny."

Claire was heartened by the news. Hopefully, she would not only have a job but meet a prospective rich husband to boot.

"Lenny seems to be settling down alright without you."

"I'm sure he is," said Claire dryly.

She couldn't have failed to notice the change in her son since arriving at the Howard household.

Very diffidently, Ellie mentioned his request to be called Lenny Howard. She had thought Claire might be angry and was surprised at Claire's amused laughter.

"I really don't care a bit," was her response. "I just thought that with his daddy dying he might want to keep his surname."

"He didn't much like his father, actually," Claire replied, bringing an end to the conversation.

She promised though that she would join them for lunch on the following Sunday, her day off. She had been quite pleased to find that she had all of Sunday and until Monday at 7 pm of every week as the restaurant closed on Sundays and re-opened on Monday evenings.

On the way home, she had bought some postcards that she noticed featured the restaurant.

She wrote to Fiona. "Well, here we are and settled on Vancouver Island. Found a good job at the restaurant shown overleaf. My new address is," and she put the address of the flat. "PS. Ellie sends greetings, though she doesn't expect you remember her. By the way, Lenny is living with them, isn't that great?" Even Claire wondered who to send the second postcard to. There really wasn't anyone else so she wrote to her brother Stewie. She wrote exactly the same on his card and posted it to Ireland and Fiona's to Sussex.

It was the first and last time she communicated for several years.

Chapter 7

Eight months had sped by. She was competent at the bar, good with customers, had made a real friend of Harris – who adored her – and she had also accumulated far more money in tips than she could have hoped with his generous advice and 'buy yourself a drink money' that she had been given.

Her only disappointment, though it was a surprisingly minor one, was that she hadn't met a rich enough man to sweep her off her feet, though several fairly rich men had offered!

Michael was delighted with her, so much so that when his wine waiter retired and his assistant wine waiter was promoted, he had no hesitation in offering Claire the job she had been training for. She was extremely competent and read up on all the wines they stocked from the fabulous clarets and burgundy to the house and vintage champagnes. They also had six white burgundies and six quality French whites. She had tasted every wine on the menu as part of her training and felt she could both advise and agree with customer choices, and when Michael invited her to the office and told her the news of her promotion she could hardly contain her delight.

Claire had changed. For the first time in her life, she felt her life had a purpose. No longer did she want to lie in bed in the mornings, she actually found herself watching the clock, longing for the time to pass so she could leave for work.

Michael explained that she would find her new job different. "The sort of people you will be looking after at the tables are equally the kind who will seldom come to the bar for a drink first. There are sometimes the awkward customer who expects and gets perfection. I know you will not let me down, Claire."

"I won't, Michael," she replied fervently, longing to escape the office and break the news to Harris.

He saw her coming and one look at her glowing, excited face told him the news he had been dreading daily, Claire was moving up and away from him at the bar. He had never had anyone working for him who had been such a delight. She had been a quick learner, was polite to the customers without being servile – remembered names and faces and greeted everyone as if they were the person she had been hoping to see.

He and Peter had talked about the changes in Claire, and they both felt they had played a major part in her transformation.

It had started early on when Harris arrived on Claire's doorstep one Sunday lunchtime with Peter in tow.

"We've come to lunch," Harris announced calmly.

Claire was horrified. "I can't cook, and I didn't invite you, and I haven't anything in. I always eat out."

Harris winked and moved aside to allow Peter to show himself. Claire had wondered about Harris, now she knew Harris was gay. She had never knowingly met a gay man, had always been ambivalent about her feelings towards them. But she liked Harris, so what, he was a person; someone who had been kind and helpful to her, rescuing her when she made the occasional mistake.

Peter was a complete contrast. Claire was reminded of old photos she had seen of a fifties film star. Rock Hudson. Peter could have stood in as a double. He was devastatingly good looking, stood about 6'4", broad shoulders, and when he smiled, he must melt women's hearts.

Fortunately, not Claire's. She was still virginal when it came to emotions of the heart. The two of them took over her kitchen, at least they started that way, then Peter gravitated to her bedroom where she was putting on her face. He sat down easily on the bed.

"Can I look at your clothes, Claire?" Claire shot him a startled look; his face had a disarming small boy expression, as if he had asked for a box of sweets.

"Help yourself," she said. Wondering what he would think of her scant array of clothes.

He moved dresses and blouses along the rail.

"Um," was all he had to say, "I haven't got money for lots of nice clothes," she found herself saying defensively. "I'm saving every penny for an operation."

"What operation?" Harris wanted to know, coming into the bedroom with the announcement that lunch was ready.

Over lunch, Claire confided her dream of a bosom reduction. The two of them looked at her critically. Harris had said something, Peter murmured, "Harris."

Claire exploded, "How dare you?"

Then the whole thing struck her as extremely funny. A couple of gays discussing her boobs. She started to laugh and soon the three of them were holding their sides until tears poured down their cheeks as they fell about.

"We'll pay," Peter said finally.

"Yes, we will," said Harris.

"One condition," Peter continued.

Claire looked blankly at them, unable to take in what they were saying.

"What condition?" she asked faintly.

"I do your new wardrobe. You'll need a complete change. I'm great with clothes, aren't I, Harris?"

"You are," Harris said, looking a little concerned on Claire's behalf.

Claire looked as if she was about to pass out.

"Are you alright, Claire?"

"I just can't believe it. You are the best friends I have ever had in my life."

It was the start of a friendship that would hang together through thick and thin and the beginning of the transformation of Claire. A few weeks later, Claire was booked into a private clinic. Harris squared it with Michael, saying he could manage for the three weeks on his own. Michael was concerned. "What operation, Claire? Are you ill?"

Claire was evasive.

"It's an operation I need, Michael," was all she would say.

When she reappeared three weeks later, he realised that the new Claire was stunning. There was no doubt that with her bosom halved in size now a 36D, her whole figure looked in better proportion.

Whilst she was in the clinic, Harris and Peter redecorated her flat. Peter made new curtains. He loved sewing, and together they filled her wardrobe with a new set of expensive-looking and beautifully-cut clothes. She was 'family' as far as they were concerned, and they wanted nothing more than to spoil and pamper her.

The operation had been a painful experience, but as she surveyed the new 'her' in the clinic's full-length mirror, she knew, beyond a shadow of a doubt, she had made the right decision.

When they brought her back to the flat, she thought at first they had bought her to the wrong place. It was transformed. The sofa had new covers, with cushions piled high. New matching curtains fluttered at the window. There were flowers everywhere. New pictures hung on newly papered walls. They had even bought new goose down filled pillows for her bed and as she lay gratefully back on them, her eyes were drawn to the open cupboard where she could see item upon item that she had never seen before. They fussed over her like parents of an only child and finally, reluctantly, saying they would be back first thing in the morning. They kissed her gently before heading home.

The shrill, unattractive sound of the telephone jolted her out of sleep. Gingerly, she sat up. The stitches still pulled and the effect of the last painkiller was wearing off. She picked up the phone, cursing whoever it was. Who was ringing at 3:00 am in the morning?

It was Fiona, ringing from England. She detected the sleepiness in her sister's voice.

"I'm sorry, Claire, did I wake you?"

"Never mind," Claire said, surfacing now as the surprise of hearing Fiona jerked her awake. "Whatever is it, Fiona?"

"I thought you should know as soon as possible that I received a letter from a clergyman in Edinburgh who had just taken the funeral."

"Funeral?" Claire's mind was still slightly fuddled with the effects of the painkillers and sleep, making clarity of thinking difficult.

"Mr Lennard, your husband, Claire, he's dead."

There was a silence as the news gradually penetrated.

Len is dead. He really was dead. She really was a widow now. She must tell Lenny, as soon as possible.

"Are you there?" Fiona asked.

"How did they track you down?" was Claire's response, though in truth she wasn't really interested.

"I'm quite well known," Fiona answered gently. "And a neighbour apparently told the vicar I was your sister. What a good job you had sent me your address."

The sisters talked for a few more minutes. Then Claire was alone with her thoughts. Len was dead. If she could have danced around the room, she would have done; instead, she lay back in her soft pillows and let her mind wander back to those strange childhood days. She thought of her mother in the wheelchair. She tried hard to remember her father, but her memories were just of a bedroom and a figure in bed. Then a grave and Fiona holding her hand. She remembered looking up and seeing Stewie crying and wondering why. She remembered looking across the grave to where her mother sat in her wheelchair. She had MS and had been in a wheelchair it seemed forever. The man standing behind her had been a stranger to Claire. Tall, dark and mysterious looking. He soon came to live with them and Fiona hated him from the first. Claire hated Len once too, but she forgot that as she grew older and then when mummy died, it seemed fine to take her place and soon she married him when she was only 18.

Well, she thought, *that was the past.*

Now, I have a future, a real future with a career and friends, but her mind forced her to acknowledge Lenny. She only saw him once a month now, on a Sunday. She felt she 'gave up' a Sunday to visit Ellie, Hugo and Lenny. She and Lenny were more like strangers now. Lenny seemed so at home with the Howards. Needs must, she would telephone Ellie and arrange to visit on the next Sunday. That gave her five more days to recover.

Harris and Peter came twice a day and sometimes Peter, who had his own hair salon, managed to pop in an extra visit as well.

On Sunday morning, as prearranged with Ellie, she arrived by taxi in time for an early lunch. Lenny greeted her politely and allowed Claire to hug him briefly. She'd taken to hugging him, partly because she felt warmer towards him, seeing him less often, and partly because her contact with Peter and Harris was affecting her, she was becoming more tactile.

Ellie and Hugo, Claire thought, seemed a bit strained over lunch. But the conversation flowed and Claire found that when talking to one of them, she would look at the other to find herself being gravely observed.

It's my boobs, she thought to herself, *it must be – they have noticed, but don't like to say.*

In truth, neither Ellie nor Hugo had noticed, they had other, weightier things on their minds. Instead of the time alone that Claire and Lenny usually spent together, when he either took her to his room – the new one, the one which their son had used, bigger and better than the original one he had slept in, or when the weather was nice they would walk through the grounds to the foreshore and walk along the beach.

Today, Lenny asked to be excused. Claire raised an eyebrow and looked at Ellie and Hugo.

"Please, Claire, we'd like to talk to you privately."

What now, Claire thought, wondering what Lenny had done or not done or whether they wanted to change the arrangements and for Claire to have him living with her again.

"I need to talk to you, Lenny," Claire said in a sharper tone than she intended, "so don't go far off."

"I'll be in my room, Mother."

And he was gone.

A slightly uneasy silence hung over the trio and then they all started speaking together and smiled awkwardly.

"You obviously have something to say," Claire said, settling back in the dining chair. "I'm listening."

It was Hugo who, after a quick glance at Ellie, revealed the bombshell. With no preambles, no time for her to focus her thoughts, with no time to argue if she had wanted to, that is. He simply, quickly announced that they wanted to formally adopt Lenny.

To say Claire was dumbfounded would be an understatement.

Hugo continued, "With his father dead and you working all the hours there are," (they had been to the restaurant on several occasions) "we feel we could provide Lenny with a good and loving home. You would, of course," he added agreeably, "be able to visit whenever you wished, but we would want to legally adopt him through the courts."

Claire was silent. Her mind was working overtime. Whatever would she have said if Len had still been alive? Lenny would have given the game away. For once, Len had done the right thing and died.

"Well, Claire," Ellie spoke for the first time. She sounded nervous. She had no way of knowing which way her friend would go. She was sure, deep down, that Claire loved her son, but she never showed it, and Lenny had blossomed in the time he had been with them. They hadn't dared mention it to him, but the bond between them was such that they both felt Lenny wanted to stay with them and be part of their family.

"I'll have to talk to Lenny," finally Claire answered after what seemed an age to the waiting couple. "It depends on him."

"Of course, Claire. We understand that completely. Do you want to talk to him now or leave it for another visit?"

"Now, I'll talk to him now." She left the table abruptly and walked across the hall, up that wonderful curving staircase and into his room.

Lenny was sitting on his bed, reading, when his mother walked in. He looked up in surprise.

"Ellie and Hugo always knock," he said a shade defensively.

Claire could feel her irritation rising. "I'm sure Ellie and Hugo are perfect," her tone was hard. She had to acknowledge that her son liked them better than he liked her.

Probably he loved them, she thought, feeling a sudden sense of loss.

"I've news for you, Lenny," she said, sitting on the end of the bed.

"Your father is dead."

He didn't look convinced.

"Lenny, I heard a few days ago from your Aunt Fiona. She had been told by the vicar who had taken the funeral."

"I don't have to lie anymore?" No expression of sadness. No tears.

God, she thought, *he is an unfeeling little blighter*, but she added to herself, *perhaps like me – more like me than I want to admit*.

"I've more news, better news this time."

He had returned to his book.

Now he put it down.

"Yes, Mother?" he said patiently.

"You like living here, don't you?"

It was more of a statement than a question.

She watched his face change, from the withdrawn look she knew so well to a child full of excitement and then fear.

"Of course, I like it here, you are not going to take me away, are you? I won't go! I won't go!" His tone was almost frightening in this intensity.

"Lenny," Claire said quietly, "they want to adopt you."

There was a stillness in the room. A stillness in the boy. A look of wonderment passed over his face.

"They want to adopt me?" he repeated.

"Oh please, oh yes, please."

He reached for his mother's hand.

"You will let me, I can, can't I? You won't say no, Mother, please?"

The earnest expression grabbed at Claire. The iceberg that she felt sure was her heart seemed to melt a little.

For a moment, she glimpsed what it was like to be loved by a small child, but that love was not directed at her. It was an impassioned plea that she had to acknowledge was directed to Ellie and Hugo.

"I want you to be adopted by them," she said. She watched his face carefully as she spoke. For the first time ever, he looked at her really warmly. He leapt towards her and hugged her tightly so that her poor tender bosoms hurt. He ran out of the room and she could hear the progress of his feet on the marble stairs.

"Ellie, Hugo," she heard him shout joyfully as she herself reached the top of the stairs.

Claire left soon afterwards. There was no way Lenny was going on a dutiful walk along the beach and Claire herself was feeling drained. She put her exhaustion down to the close proximity of the operation and the debilitating effect of the anaesthetic. But she also knew she did feel an emotion that bordered somewhere near sadness, acknowledging that today she had lost the son she never really had.

Harris and Peter were already at the flat when she arrived. She had forgotten they were coming round to prepare supper. For once, she wished she could be alone, but in fact, she realised that alone she would have become morose and introspective. Instead, she confided in them. She told them that she hadn't been a widow until a few days ago, that Lenny was to be adopted and that she didn't understand why she felt miserable, and saying so, she promptly burst into tears.

Harris and Peter were a fortress of strength. While Harris made her a drink, Peter gently hugged her and wiped her tears with one of his impeccably clean handkerchiefs.

"What will become of me?" she moaned over and over.

Finally, their ministrations and the result of a second stronger cocktail took effect and she became almost impossibly bright.

Their talk ranged from Peter's salon to the restaurant to Claire's future career and her efforts to find a really rich husband.

Chapter 8

With a few minor hiccups, Claire's new career was progressing well. She learned to curb her impatient tendencies as customers either wouldn't or couldn't make-up their minds about what wines to drink, would ask advice and not take it, or would change their minds as soon as she produced the wines they ordered, only having to start the whole proceedings again.

There were, however, other customers who more than made up for this, charming, friendly, either knowing exactly what they wanted or taking and appreciating her advice.

She seldom saw Lenny these days. Ellie phoned her from time to time to give her news of his latest achievement, or she would send her a copy of his school report card. He had developed into an ice hockey fiend, Ellie confided, and was likely to be picked for the school team. Claire found it almost impossible to imagine. He had obviously changed more than she had thought possible. His school work too was going well and Ellie sounded happy and pleased. The adoption papers were due anytime now and Ellie wondered if Claire would like to visit on Sunday as she hadn't been for several months. She didn't want to go, the new Claire felt ashamed at her feelings. Harris and Peter scolded her.

"You must, Claire, he may not appear to need you, but he is your son, and you do owe him time."

Feeling suitably chastised, Claire took particular trouble with her appearance. Peter did her hair these days, the red had become subtle, the cut stylish, slightly shorter at the back than the sides, and falling forward on to her cheeks just at the level of the bottom of her ear lobes, with a feathered fringe providing the finishing frame to her face. Peter had also advised and helped her with her make-up, giving her lessons until her makeup was of a professional order. She looked younger, more vulnerable and extremely stylish.

Hugo could hardly take his eyes off the new Claire and his admiration did not go unnoticed by Ellie, who decided that she would be less persuasive in the future over potential visits.

To Claire's surprise, Hugo had papers for her to sign and although she would have further documents to sign in an attorney's office, the court proceedings could now go ahead. The 'Social Services Welfare' had approved of the Howards; feeling that he would have a far more stable home than with his own mother, who, when they had interviewed her, had come over as a selfish, hard woman with little or no interest in her son.

Lunch was an uncomfortable occasion. Lenny was no longer morose, but he avoided both eye contact and conversation with his mother and was almost overly conversational with Ellie and Hugo, who Claire noticed he once or twice called Mum and Dad, then looked over in confusion as it was obviously a 'family' secret.

Ellie felt an enormous sense of relief when Claire left. With Claire gone, Lenny returned to being her son again and Hugo started to behave more normally. She hadn't been able to believe his secret glances at her old friend, but she had to admit Claire seemed almost a different person from the brash, tartish looking girl who had arrived unannounced only 12 months earlier.

Chapter 9

"Kostas is in town." Claire heard Michael telling Harris.

"I wonder who he will have for company when he comes in tonight."

Claire was intrigued, there was something unusual in Michael's tone.

"Who is Kostas?" she wanted to know.

"Ah," said Michael, "you might well ask. Kostas, or Constantine Stavros Papadofulas, is Greek, very rich, had three wives, arrives once or twice a year in his yacht and usually has a girl in tow. He spends a lot – and I mean a lot – of money here. He can be very charming, but I have heard he can be unpleasant too, though I have to say, in all fairness, I've never seen anything but the charm, and he always chooses the best wines and spends more in one evening than most of our customers do in six visits."

Claire was impressed and immediately decided that she would serve his table. Perhaps, this was the man she had been waiting for.

That evening, she dressed with particular care, choosing one of the two black suits chosen for her by Peter. Her favourite one had deep-blue twin back satin cuffs and matching collar. Apart from this the outfit was stark in its simplicity and had caused several raised eyebrows amongst some of the wealthier female customers who knew a thing or two about quality clothes. Claire was impervious to this; however, all she knew was that Peter had great taste in clothes, that they fitted perfectly, and she felt good in them.

She washed her hair and blow-dried it, made up with even more care than usual and gave herself a quick spray of her favourite Black Opium. Tonight, she was determined that she would make this Kostas notice her – Paul had already checked the table. Impervious to Claire's pleas, he said he would attend the table. Kostas would expect the head sommelier, not his assistant. Knowing there was nothing to be gained from arguing except causing an atmosphere between them, Claire kept her counsel and made her own plans.

She was busy at another table and was only aware of Kostas' arrival by the sensation of activity behind her. She was particularly attentive to her own customers who were charmed by her helpfulness and concern in their choosing of the wines for their meal. Claire didn't glance once in the direction of the Kostas' table although it took a great deal of willpower not to do so. Discreetly, as she came out of the wine store with the starter wine for her table, she cast a covert glance at the Kostas table. To her annoyance, Kostas was looking at her and raised an eyebrow in her direction. She could feel herself flush, partly with annoyance at being spotted, and partly because she felt disadvantaged. She didn't make the mistake of looking that way again, although she felt his eyes boring into her back. He was a big man, not in height but in breadth. He was probably only about 5' 6", but he was a man who obviously enjoyed good food and wine as much as he enjoyed women, judging by Michael's earlier comments. The evening seemed unbearably long. For the first time, Claire willed customers to leave early, particularly Kostas and his party.

The party consisted of two other people: a man of around 30 to 40 and a young woman who looked no more than 20. She had blonde hair that reached halfway down her back and a fringe so long it almost covered her eyes. Once Claire heard a tinkling laugh from her, but as she passed close to the table at intervals during that long evening, it was the murmur of male voices that seemed to predominate.

Finally, finally, only Kostas and his party were there. Claire disappeared to the wine store to update her itinerary, glad now that she had a real reason not to go into the restaurant again. She heard the door close and when she heard Michael with his bunch of keys starting the locking up, she came back into the dining room.

Michael looked up from his key turning and smiled at her.

"Kostas has asked that you look after his wines tomorrow evening," he said. "You obviously made an impression."

Claire smiled, but she could feel a tightening of her stomach muscles and her heart seemed to miss a beat. This was what she wanted, yet she felt suddenly, unexpectedly afraid.

Once again, she dressed with particular care, wearing the second suit Peter had chosen. This time, the turn-back satin cuffs and collar were of deep turquoise, and she made up her eyes using the exact colour on her eyelids, but very discreetly. She stood back from the mirror and looked at herself dispassionately. How she had changed. Her sister wouldn't recognise her now. She remembered the look on Fiona's face when they had met up in London after so many years of not seeing each other. Fiona had looked very much the lady and now the new Claire would, she felt sure, have met with nothing but approval from her older sister.

Why she was thinking about Fiona suddenly out of the blue, she didn't know. Perhaps it was because she was feeling a little unsure about what was going to happen between her and Kostas and something was going to happen of that, she was sure.

Kostas, getting ready for dinner in his cabin, gave her a passing thought. He was already bored with Binny the blonde, though he was still 'enjoying' her in his own inimitable way. He looked at himself in the mirror and wished, not for the first time, that he was less stocky. He had never aspired to film star looks. He knew full well that money could buy anything he needed or wanted. The only regret he had in his life was that his mother had died so unexpectedly. She was probably the only person he had ever loved but also definitely the only person he had ever respected.

He thought back to his childhood in Assos on Cephalonia. A small village with a tight-knit community. His parents had the only big house. It was right on the square, its gardens enclosed within high walls and the locals could only look through the double wrought iron gate and see for themselves the well-trimmed and green lawns and the abundance of flowers. Roses had been his mother's favourite flowers. The heavy scented roses whose smell still made him feel like a child on his mother's knee. His father had been a shadowy figure, always away somewhere or another on one business venture after another. He owned ships, land and properties in so many different countries that Kostas had not yet had time to even visit them all himself.

No doubt, he thought wryly, *servants were having a high old time enjoying living off the Papadofulas family.*

One day, Kostas vowed, *not for the first time, I will arrive at each place unannounced and catch them out.*

It gave him a warm feeling. To be able to catch someone at a disadvantage provided him with the advantage which was what he not only wanted from life, but expected too.

Binny, he thought of her momentarily again, *tonight would be the last night.*

He had other plans after that.

He smiled at himself in the mirror and called for 'Frederick'. Frederick was an employee. Quite an exceptional employee. He performed whatever task Kostas demanded, either pleasant or unpleasant. Frederick both admired and hated Kostas in almost equal proportions but he knew that if push came to shove, he would support Kostas completely. He heard 'his master's voice' and, as ever, knocked, then walked straight into the room.

Kostas turned from the mirror. His face was, as ever when they were in private, unsmiling. Kostas reserved his rare smiles for when he wanted to charm some woman. He never wasted them on deals. People either did what he wanted or Kostas walked away.

"Binny," he said in a tone that was as familiar as it was expected. "Binny must go." Frederick nodded, unsurprised.

"When?"

"Tomorrow morning," Kostas spoke unemotionally.

He was never touched, ever. Frederick couldn't help thinking, wondering at the same time, if he ever would be. He couldn't really imagine this happening but he was unsurprised at Binny's abrupt dismissal. He would do the usual, give her a gold watch and depending on the state she was in, give her an envelope stuffed with dollars. It usually worked alright; there was no reason to assume she would be any different from the rest.

Kostas changed his tie. He always got a tinge of excitement when a new woman was to be taken. He always thought of it in these terms.

He had seen her look in his direction. He had noticed her deliberately avoiding his eyes afterwards. An English bitch would be a change. His smile wasn't pleasant as he thought of her. She might take a little time to land, but that was the fun, once he had her then she would, like all the others, become a bore. He cursed himself again for the marriages, when briefly he had thought that these women could perhaps match up to his mother. Now, he knew, no one could do that. They were just bitches on heat and money made them dance for him.

Claire would have been horrified had she known what was going on in the mind of the man she was dressing so precisely for. But innocence is sometimes a blessing, and she believed that she and she alone would call the shots. She was excited, very excited and made her way to the restaurant with her heart seeming to pound louder at every step she took. Michael was waiting for her.

"Claire," he began. "Kostas can be very difficult. I can, if you want, refuse to let you look after his wines tonight. He could well be a challenge to you. I have seen him reduce grown men to tears before now. He has a way with his tongue and his manner."

Claire drew herself up and looked him straight in the eye. "Michael, you have always said you had confidence in me. You either have or you haven't. I am your second sommelier. If I have a problem I can't solve, which is unlikely, I shall consult Harris. Otherwise, whatever he throws at me, I shall cope."

Michael nodded, but he still looked a little anxious.

"So be it," he said quietly, shrugging his shoulders.

Kostas arrived at 9 pm. As it happened, that was the first problem of the evening. Claire was busy at an adjacent table when they had called for more wine but wanted to try something different. She couldn't just leave them and she certainly wasn't prepared to leave them in the middle of an order, so she turned her back quite deliberately on the Kostas party. She heard

62

Michael talking smoothly. The waiter came over with menus which were waved away.

"Either she attends to us now," Claire heard him say, "or we leave."

Fortunately, the dilemma at Claire's table was solved as they chose a dessert wine to go with the pavlovas. She walked purposefully towards the wine store and collected the dessert wine, walked decisively back to the client, keeping her eyes averted from the Kostas table, though she heard his drumming fingers impatiently tapping the table.

Apparently unconcerned, though with her heart beating in an irregular fashion, she opened and poured a small quantity of the mellow golden wine for the table's host. He smiled agreeably at her and inclined his head for her to pour for his three guests. Then, and only then, did she allow herself to turn towards the Kostas table, where Kostas himself glared uncompromisingly at her.

His tone, when he spoke, was brusque! "At last. The service here is not what it used to be."

Claire produced the wine list, but he waved it away with an impatient hand.

"Don't bother me with that," he said, his voice rude and gruff. "I know you will have something special tucked away. Cost doesn't matter, you understand?"

Claire smiled as pleasantly as she could, though she could feel anger rising in her. Whatever she did, she must not lose her temper that would play right into his hands.

"Sir, whatever we have is on our wine list. May I point out, however, that the white Burgundy, a very special wine and extremely expensive, is now down to very few bottles. May I recommend you have this with your starter, which I believe is—"

"Fish," he exploded before she could finish her sentence. "You really think that would go well? Where did they train you, girl?"

Claire swallowed hard. "I believe you would find that the perfect choice," she said, controlling a threatening quiver.

Somewhat ungraciously, he inclined his head and waved his hand at her as if dismissed. The blonde sitting next to him had watched wide eyed as Claire stood her ground. She always acquiesced to everything Kostas said or did, and she wished she knew how to stand up to him, or had the guts to walk way. But she had come from nowhere. She had caught his eye in a nightclub where she was a dancer, and he had told her she was not very pretty, but she had long slim legs of which he approved. She always agreed to his demands and sometimes aggressive behaviour. Tonight, he had told her that her time was nearly up, though, and she had quietly been round the yacht, picking up the odd small trinket which she could sell at a later date. Frederick, being the eyes and ears of his master, had, of course, noticed and said nothing, but before he handed her the envelope of dollars in the morning, he would make sure she was relieved of her spoils. For now, though, Kostas required another night of pleasure, so nothing was said to mar that.

Finally, Claire was able to escape to the kitchen, where she covered her face with her hands. Her cheeks glowed with a mixture of embarrassment and anger, and only the fact that she needed and liked the job, adored Michael and everyone she worked with, made her go back again and again to that horrible man's table.

And, she thought bitterly, *this was the man I was planning to 'snare'. What a rattlesnake!*

Finally, the evening was over. Claire was surprised when Michael called her into the office.

"Have I done something wrong, Michael? Did I offend Kostas?"

"Far from it," he grinned as he handed her a $200 note. "For you."

"How astonishing! And he was so rude, I thought he hated me."

Michael smiled, "You did well, Claire. He was testing you. I couldn't warn you in advance because I never know how he is going to react, but you did well under very difficult circumstances."

Claire's mood changed. She had coped with Kostas, their most difficult customer. What's more, he had left her the biggest tip that she had so far received. She put on her coat, went to talk

64

briefly to Harris and then almost ran home and was asleep as her head touched the pillow.

Kostas was angry. He had given Claire a reasonable tip, but he was cross that he had not managed to get under her skin. Her expression had remained calm, her attitude unflappable. He was disappointed. He had reduced many a similar female to tears and then despised them so. Although he was irritated, he was also a little intrigued. She might be a little more of a challenge and that made life a little more interesting.

Once again, Claire dressed with particular attention to detail; tonight, though, more for her own satisfaction. Would Kostas be there? So, what? If he was, she would remain as calm on the surface as she had the previous evening.

She need not have worried. Tonight, Kostas arrived full of beaming smiles. He was accompanied tonight only by Frederick. Of Binny, there was no sign. Binny had been correct in her reading of the signs and at lunchtime, Kostas had told her in a pre-emptory fashion to pack and go.

"The jewels stay here," he told her. "All of them."

His tone sounded sufficiently fierce to worry Binny. She had so hoped to sneak perhaps a gold bracelet or a ring or two in her bags, but she felt sure Kostas would somehow guess and would frighten her again.

He had frightened her on several occasions, usually when they made 'love'.

It was, thought Binny, *hardly making love; it was often brutal, always insensitive.*

She felt used and abused.

But he had been generous.

Her wardrobe of new clothes was her own and the pay-off had been more than she hoped.

"But," he had told her after Frederick had handed her the envelope, "you do not, under any circumstances, discuss your time with me. Should you be so foolish, you will regret it, I promise you."

The threat was barely veiled.

Binny, unable to speak, had merely nodded; suddenly glad to be leaving Kostas and the yacht.

When Frederick searched her luggage again, she felt mortified, but she was almost glad he had found the items she had stashed away earlier. This time, he found nothing.

He escorted her down the gang-plank and as she stood on the quay in the bright sunshine, with people meandering past looking enviously at the yacht, Frederick repeated what Kostas had said. She heard menace in his tone too and vowed to keep silent. There were things she had seen and heard on board the yacht and elsewhere that could make her a fortune. But what was money if she was dead? And she believed she could be if she didn't heed the warnings.

Claire once again offered the wine menu. Once again, it was waved away, but this time with an apparently kindly smile.

"Your choice, my dear. I leave it to your innate good taste."

Claire smiled with pleasure; he was not so bad after all. The evening went well. The food was to his taste, the wines, he informed her, chilled to perfection. Not cold but cold enough for the full flavour to be enjoyed. At the end of the evening, he handed her another $200. Claire hesitated for a moment, then decided to accept the money. He had plenty. He was pleased with the service, and he was pleased with her. He also gave her an invitation to join him and Frederick at the yacht for a nightcap when the restaurant closed.

Once, Claire would have said an immediate yes. But the new, more mature, more sophisticated Claire held back. "I'm sorry, I have other plans. Perhaps another time."

If Kostas was annoyed, he didn't show it.

"Of course," he smiled smoothly. "Another time."

Chapter 10

He didn't come every evening and Claire found herself feeling disappointed when he didn't show. There was something about the man that both frightened and attracted her. She knew that he was the rich man she had been looking for, but she also knew from both Harris and Peter that he used women and discharged them. His three marriages had been quite stormy affairs. His second wife had died in rather mysterious circumstances, just disappearing off the yacht during a night sail and not being missed until the following morning when a thorough search was made. Her mutilated body was found weeks later. Ugly rumours abounded, but the authorities accepted that the mutilations were caused by rocks and sharks and no further enquiries were made. He married a month after the enquiry, but the marriage floundered almost immediately and since then he had just had a series of young nubile females coming and going in his life.

Kostas felt that Claire was being difficult, but the more evasive she became, the more interested he was in her.

He invited her to go sailing for a few days.

"I'm sure you are due a holiday," he suavely told her. "And if not, then I will arrange it with Michael. Nothing is impossible."

Claire implored Michael not to give in to Kostas' invitation until she was ready. Michael readily agreed, not at all sure that he wanted his Claire, as he now thought of her, involved with Kostas. Claire rang Ellie and invited herself for a couple of days. Surprisingly, she wanted to see Lenny. He didn't feel like her son anymore. But then, he never really had. But whereas when she was responsible for him, he bored her, now she felt more like a distant aunt showing interest in a nephew.

If Ellie was surprised at the request, she was polite enough not to show it. It was agreed that Claire would arrive on the following Sunday in time for lunch and leave again on Tuesday.

Michael suggested that she have three to four days and although she agreed, she only wanted to stay with Ellie and Hugo for part of the time, feeling it would be pleasant to have a bit of space for herself.

Chapter 11

Ellie and Hugo made her feel very welcome. Any strain or stress that there had been prior to the adoption was well past. Lenny was their son, so much so that they found it hard to imagine life before. He was happy and settled at school. He had fitted in and found himself a group of friends. He had two parents, albeit adoptive parents, who made no secret of the fact that they loved him dearly and he responded by opening up, showing them affection, sharing his thoughts and dreams. He was even relaxed now about Claire's proposed visit. His feelings about her were no longer ambivalent. She had been a lousy mother, but he had matured enough to recognise it was not totally her fault. She had hardly been 'mothered' except by her sister, and she had had no rational instinct or inclination that way.

He even felt strangely grateful to her in an odd sort of way. She had, after all, taken him away from the greyness of Edinburgh and the unfriendliness of his school companions. She had even found new parents for him and he felt gratitude, and even affection, towards her.

Lenny had changed. He was no longer the sullen ten-year-old with a chip on his shoulder, but a happy, cheerful, outgoing Canadian boy who had become even more Canadian than his classmates, so determined was he to fit in and belong.

His greeting to Claire when she arrived took her quite by surprise. He had taken on board the more tactile behaviour of his adoptive parents, and he actually hugged her.

"Hi, Claire," had been his opening remark on seeing her.

Claire noticed she was no longer 'mother' and decided it was a lot more comfortable to be Claire.

It was a jolly Sunday lunch, so different from the last one they had shared, when Hugo had gawped at the 'new Claire'.

Ellie had felt threatened by her presence in relation to Lenny, and Lenny had just hated her being there. Claire saw they were a solid family unit now and responded in kind, feeling comfortable with Ellie again and pleased that Hugo's feelings had obviously calmed down.

Lenny kept them all laughing with lively tales about his friends, baseball, riding, which he had taken up, and sailing, of which he had become a passionate devotee, sailing every weekend with 'Dad', as he now easily and comfortably called Hugo.

Claire looked at the three of them warmly.

How they had all changed, but most especially herself and Lenny.

She resolved to write to Fiona and tell her all her news.

Really, had it not been for her sister's generosity, she wouldn't be here at all.

The time passed all too quickly.

Claire responded to their questions about her work, she even mentioned Kostas.

"Now there is a man to watch," Hugo said seriously.

"I know," Claire replied.

"But I am playing him my way, not his."

"Do be careful, Claire," Ellie sounded genuinely concerned. "He has a strange reputation, you know."

"I'm a big girl, Ellie, I can take care of myself."

Ellie looked doubtful.

Lenny looked interested. "Who is Kostas?" he wanted to know.

"Just a Greek, quite a wealthy Greek."

"Beware of Greeks, bearing gifts," the boy said so solemnly that they all burst out laughing.

Lenny looked quite hurt.

"That's what I heard," he said defensively.

Claire smiled at him.

"I'll bear it in mind, Lenny. Thank you for your concern."

It was thoughts like these that she took away with her when they said their goodbyes. Lenny hugged her warmly, and she hugged him back. She knew it would be a while before they saw each other again. There was no need to visit Lenny. He was happy. Ellie and Hugo were happy and Claire knew that she was happy too. It was a good feeling and one, she acknowledged, she had not felt very often in her life.

Chapter 12

Once back in the flat, she unpacked her small bag and left a message on Harris and Peter's voicemail to let them know she was back. Then, surprising herself, she put on a pair of white trousers and a T-shirt and walked to the harbour. Kostas' yacht was gone. The bird had flown. Claire almost stamped her foot in annoyance. She had played him too long. He had moved to other waters.

Frowning, she turned around to head back the way she had come, almost bumping into someone as she turned.

"I'm sorry," she began apologetically without looking at the person blocking her way.

"And I thought you were away," Kostas said, smiling a trifle wryly.

"And I thought you had left," she responded, not realising that her tone indicated her disappointment.

Kostas smiled inwardly. It had been a good idea of Frederick's to move the yacht; the mouse had nibbled at the bait. Now he felt he would be able to play the game as he always did.

"My staff gets bored." He said by way of explanation, "So I send the yacht out for an hour or two, and they play at being sailors."

He laughed as he spoke and Claire wasn't sure that it was a particularly kindly laugh, but she laughed with him anyway.

He put his arm through hers. "I know of a perfect place for a drink," he said. "It is small, only a select membership and of course their guests. You will come, won't you?"

It was more of a statement than a question and Claire found herself nodding her assent. His grip on her arm was strong; a little anticipating shiver went through her body. She was taking the very first step in the next part of her life, and she knew she would need all her wits about her.

The club was as Kostas described: small, select discreet and quiet. They sat in one of the booths placed along the walls in the centre of the room. A round table, on which rested one of the most beautiful flower arrangements Claire had ever seen. Its object was to provide privacy so that in every booth each couple were able to talk in apparent privacy. Soft music provided the background and as they sat, two balloons of brandy were placed in front of them.

Claire looked surprised, remembering Kostas' normal behaviour over wines. He noticed her surprised look and said, "They know I always drink brandy here, if you would like something else?" Claire shook her head.

"Brandy will be fine," she said, resolving to sip very slowly and make it last as long as possible.

It was not a favourite drink of hers, but more importantly, she wanted to be clear headed – she was almost sure that Kostas had further plans for the evening and they might not coincide with hers.

If Kostas was surprised at the small quantity of brandy that his guest consumed, he didn't comment. He ordered another one for himself and with it came a small plate of delicious hors d'oeuvres. Claire enjoyed the delectable nibbles, still making her brandy last and last.

Finally, Kostas burst out laughing. "Well, Madam," he said, "you look like becoming one of the least expensive women in my life."

"Am I in your life, Kostas?"

Their eyes met and held.

She felt an intense power emanating from him. She felt both fascinated and repelled. He had a dark side to him, but in a way that made him even more of a challenge, even more interesting.

"The yacht will be back at the Marina," he said, still looking at her.

She lowered her eyes. This would be the difficult part. She was taking a risk. She could lose before she won.

"I'm not coming to the yacht, Kostas."

The silence was deafening. She could only hear the thump thump of her heart. It was as if their booth with its soft leather seats was in an empty space. She watched his expression anxiously. She saw surprise, annoyance, amusement and finally after what seemed like an eternity, he laughed. He went on laughing for several moments then abruptly stopped and looked her squarely in the face again.

"So," he said softly. "Little Claire is going to play hard to get."

"I don't know what you mean," she began a shade indignantly.

But she did, and he knew she did.

"I don't mind playing games, if that is what you want."

There was a quality in his voice she recognised from far off. Len used to speak to Fiona like that, tauntingly slightly cruel, but she had dealt with Len. He had, apart from the times he hit her, been controllable, and she had left him when living with him was too much. She could handle this Greek. Who was he to think he could make her walk his way? She was older and wiser. She had grown up a lot. Harris and Peter had seen to that. They had warned her about playing with fire, but they also gave her good advice when it became clear that that was what she proposed to do.

"Hold back," they said. "Make him wait. Most women fall into his lap. The more you keep him waiting, the more he will want you, and the only way you go to him is marriage. Right, Claire? Marriage."

Claire had listened and learned. She had been an eager pupil, and she followed their advice. Kostas would have to wait until she was ready to give him what he wanted.

If Kostas had been able to read Claire's mind, he would have got up from the table and left her abruptly, but, fortunately, he could not. He finally smiled in a conciliatory way. If she wanted to play games, he would enjoy playing her even more, like the big fish he fished for in his beautiful Ionian Sea. He was not a patient man, but this time he would be patient, for a short while anyway.

Chapter 13

The next few weeks were full of surprises and uncertainties. Claire worked as usual at the restaurant. Kostas came for dinner from time to time, but not, according to Michael, as much as usual.

"What have you done to my best paying customer?" Michael wanted to know.

Claire could only shrug her shoulders.

Kostas was playing her at her own game, and he was probably better at it than she was. His yacht had disappeared one morning and stayed away for a week.

Just when Claire had decided he had lost interest, there was a knock on the door.

She had just arrived home from a particularly boring evening in the restaurant and when the knock came, she almost didn't bother to answer it. But it could be Harris or Peter and for them she would answer any door, whatever the time.

It was neither Harris nor Peter.

Frederick stood there with a small package in his hand. "I'm sorry, it's so late," he began, "but Constantine wanted to be sure you received this tonight."

He handed over a small square box wrapped in black tissue paper and tied with a narrow gold ribbon.

Frederick was the last person she was expecting to see. She automatically invited him in, but fortunately, he declined. "No, Miss Claire, I am just the messenger," and with that he turned away and walked to the lift.

Intrigued, Claire sat on the sofa and opened the small package. Under the wrapping and resting on the lid of the box was a small card which read:

Claire, the first gift of many.
Kostas.

She opened the box and there, lying in its velvet nest, was a slender gold bracelet, around which small gems were placed, each surrounded by tiny diamonds.

It was the most beautiful thing she had ever seen.

For a moment, she could not even bring herself to touch it. Then she lifted it carefully out of the box and held it.

For several moments, she was tempted, seriously tempted, but she knew what she had to do. She put it back, trying to put it exactly as she had first seen it. Walking to the bedroom, she put it on her bedside table so that before she fell asleep, she could take one final look.

In the morning, her eyes flew to her side table. Had she imagined the whole thing or had she really held such an exquisite piece in her hands?

True, there it was, wickedly winking at her, beguilingly appealing to be taken up and rested on warm, soft skin.

She leaned over and closed the lid and before she could be tempted further, she repacked it again. Harris and Peter would be proud of her. She could not wait to return the wretched thing to Kostas. Now she began to feel annoyed. How dare he try and buy her? She has changed more than she knew. There was a time when she would have delightedly accepted it, whatever that acceptance entailed. No, she was out for bigger stakes now. She would not be trapped so easily. If Kostas was surprised to receive his gift back, delivered by private messenger, he never let Claire know how he felt. He read her brief note carefully and gave a quiet, satisfied smile. He was enjoying playing this 'little fish'.

That evening, Kostas was in the restaurant again. Henry served his table and received the usual tip. Claire was busy, but not busy enough to fail to see there was a new, young blonde accompanying Kostas and Frederick. It was sad, she thought, the relationship between Kostas and Frederick, it was somewhere between master, servant and friendship. Michael said Frederick had been with Kostas for years. There had been some scandal; he didn't know the details, but supposedly Frederick, in his capacity as a lawyer, had helped with some difficulties to such an extent that he had remained ever after in Kostas' employ. For outsiders their relationship was sometimes hard to fathom.

Kostas left shortly after 11 pm with not a glance in Claire's direction. She couldn't help feeling a shade despondent, she had blown it. He was no longer going to pursue her. Her sense of disappointment surprised even her. She confided to Harris, as she spent a moment by the bar.

He smiled. "He'll be back, Claire, your big fish is tempted by the bait, but he is not used to being played at his own game."

Claire shrugged her shoulders. "Maybe," she answered with a smile. "But maybe not."

She did not have to wait long. Before she left, Michael handed her a note. It was from Kostas. She recognised the writing on the envelope.

"Please be careful, Claire, my dear," Michael said. "You are playing with fire. Kostas can be dangerous!"

Claire felt a shiver down her spine and at the same moment her heart seemed to miss a beat. She felt afraid, excited and stimulated – each emotion as powerful as the one preceding it.

Once in the wine store, she tore open the envelope.

My car is waiting for you outside, please allow my driver to bring you to the yacht for a nightcap. Martine, my little friend, will be with us. Later, if you wish, my driver will drive you home, or you may stay on board overnight (everything you might need will be in your cabin). If you are unable to come tonight, please tell my driver, and he will drive you home. I hope this is not the case - Kostas.

What to do? She wanted to go. If she stuck to her new principals, then surely it would be alright. She would have a drink. She might even stay overnight, tomorrow, being Sunday, was her day off.

Had he realised this? she wondered.

Probably. He was nobody's fool.

Uncertain as to why, she sought out Harris ostensibly to say goodnight, but she took the opportunity to show him the note. She watched his face whilst he read it. His doubts and fears for her showed clearly. How good it was to be cared for.

"You're going?" It was not so much a question as a statement.

She nodded.

"Will you stay overnight?"

"I don't know, Mother Hen," Claire laughed as she spoke but to her it sounded rather hollow. She felt a coldness clutching her heart – but it was now or never. She leaned over the bar and kissed him lightly.

"Bye, Harris darling, think of me."

"I most certainly will," he responded in a rather graver tone than he had intended.

The limousine and smartly dressed chauffeur were exactly outside the door. The place was always reserved by Michael for a special guest, even occasional European Royals.

Tonight, Kostas unsurprisingly had the pride of place, or rather his car had. Primed, the chauffeur opened the door as she approached, obviously been given a description, she thought wryly, wishing she could have heard how Kostas described her. The car smelt of beautifully soft leather and the lingering aroma of Kostas' last cigar.

In a short while, they had glided to a smooth stop on the quay side adjacent to 'The Pandora'. Claire had winced slightly when she had first seen the name. What hidden secrets did it hold? Was it as full of dangers lurking within as had been in the legendary Pandora's Box?

Well, perhaps she was about to find out.

Frederick, the ubiquitous Frederick, was at the top of the stairway to meet her. No gang plank to this ship – nothing so mundane.

"Miss Claire, we are delighted you have been able to join us."

Was this the use of the royal 'we' or was he, she wondered, speaking for Kostas as well as himself. He led her along the side of the yacht to the aft (as she learned to call it) where Kostas, looking relaxed, reclined on a cushion filled sofa, brandy in one hand, cigar in the other and was apparently listening as the blonde, Martine, chattered in an incessant stream like a tumbling waterfall.

As Claire came into view, and with surprising agility for a man of his size, Kostas deposited the brandy on the table in front of him and sprang to his feet.

"My dear Claire, we are so delighted that you have decided to join us."

That 'we' again, she noticed.

Martine looked a bit sulky and petulant, being interrupted so rudely, though she had been aware that Kostas seldom actually listened to anything she said.

Claire held out her hand in response to Kostas. He didn't take it but drew her hand to his lips and kissed it in a slow lingering way, his eyes all the time holding hers as if in a challenge.

Claire withdrew her hand and laughed lightly to try to lessen the charged atmosphere that seemed to surround her. Martine stood up, shaking her long blonde hair as she did so.

Rather like a pony tossing his mane, Claire thought.

God, she was young.

Kostas really was a devil, taking these young girls as he did.

However, she reminded herself that was not her problem. She held out her hand to shake Martine's, but the girl tossed her head again, this time somewhat disdainfully.

"You're that waitress person, aren't you, from the restaurant?"

For a moment, the old Claire could have slapped her face, but the new, sleek, well-groomed well-schooled Claire simply smiled back.

"I work at the restaurant," she said. "Not exactly as a waitress, but that's alright."

Kostas, who had looked as if he was about to explode, looked at Claire again, once again their eyes meeting and holding.

She is special, he was thinking.

She smiled, still holding his eyes for another moment, then dropped easily into a chair and accepted the proffered drink from Frederick.

The next two hours passed in idle chat whilst at intervals one of the crew bought small plates of delectable edibles, tiny choux pastry horns with prawns and a delicious dressing. Little patties stuffed with smoked salmon and bowls of caviar accompanied by crispbread, or, as Kostas did, eaten neat with a teaspoon!

Martine was almost asleep, bored by the conversation. Claire, glancing at her watch, was surprised to find it was almost 2 am.

She stood up as she glanced. "I have overstayed my welcome. Please, will you ask your driver to take me home?"

She saw a look between the two men.

It was Frederick who spoke as smoothly as ever.

"Miss Claire, it's too late, why don't I show you to one of the guest cabins."

"Oh good, she's going," said Martine, waking up. "Come on, Kostas, take me to bed-e-byes."

Staking her claim, Claire thought, inwardly smiling at Martine's clumsy behaviours and recognising something of herself as was.

Claire hesitated for only a moment. Kostas would be no trouble, and why not, it would certainly be easier to stay than go.

Before she realised it, she was being led down the companion way and along a corridor – at the far end, there were double doors.

Frederick waved in their general direction, 'Kostas Suite', before opening a door halfway along the wide corridor.

Claire was amazed first at the width of the corridor, so beautifully lit and carpeted, it was as if she was in a hotel, nothing could have prepared her for the size and luxury of this boat.

Frederick flung open the door, and she had to stifle a gasp. A huge double bed took pride of place – a few comfortable looking chairs and sofa, a cupboard covering one wall which Frederick opened to reveal several silk nightgowns in various tones and a pair of white silk pyjamas. Also, she noted, white linen trousers and several different tops.

Frederick indicated these. "For the morning," he said matter-of-factly, as if she usually was provided with clothes when she went away overnight.

A door slightly ajar, Frederick indicated, was her bathroom. "Please, Miss Claire, ring if there's anything you need at any time. Breakfast is served at 8:30 am. Kostas does like guests to be on time. Would you like coffee or tea at 8 o'clock?"

"Coffee would be lovely."

She was alone, smooth as ever. Frederick had nodded a goodnight and closed the door silently behind him. She noticed the key and turned it, and as if to reassure herself, she pushed one of the chairs in front of the door as well.

Then suddenly feeling incredibly tired, she stepped out of her clothes and took the pyjamas from the wardrobe. She, who never wore pyjamas! The feel of the silk and the perfect fit made her smile. Kostas again. Clever man, she had to acknowledge that!

The bathroom was, of course, equally beautifully appointed. Gold taps. Gold shower head. The bath taps were shaped like dolphins as was the shower head and as she felt the water pouring over her, she wondered if this boat, this luxury would one day be her home.

After showering, and now unsurprised by anything, she found body lotion, talc and her favourite perfume. Once again, clever man crossed her mind. The pyjamas slid over her body like a second skin, touching her gently and of course, as she had surmised, they were the perfect fit. She checked the door, which was still firmly locked, then in a momentary panic, looked carefully around the room to ensure there was no other less obvious way in. Having satisfied herself, she pulled back the covers. Of course, she should have known. The sheets were of the palest rose silk and as she lay down she knew she had never known such comfort.

For a few moments, she tried to imagine a life permanently at this level but Morpheus overtook her and she went into a deep and dreamless sleep. From somewhere far away, she heard knocking, then more knocking. Guiltily, she leapt out of bed and moved the chair and unlocked the door as silently as she could before running back to the bed and settling herself momentarily before calling, "Come in."

To her relief, it was one of the crew, not Frederick, carrying a tray with a small silver teapot, cup and saucer, lemon slices and milk.

When he had deposited it carefully on her side table, he said in (what she presumed was heavily-accented Greek voice), "Mr Papadofulas says breakfast at 8:30."

Claire nodded and as soon as he had left the room, she poured some tea and then headed for the bathroom, leaving it to cool.

After washing and brushing her teeth, she opened the wardrobe, looking closely at the garments hanging there. Her black suit seemed totally unsuitable on the Sunday morning. She touched the white linen trousers.

"Why not," she said out loud.

Of course, they fitted perfectly as did the navy Ferragamo shoes and the navy-and-white sweater. She looked in the full-length mirror and was not displeased then back to the dressing table where she had noticed brushes and combs and a range of makeup. She brushed her hair well then gave it a quick hairspray. She always carried basic make-up needs in her handbag so she used her own moisturiser and lightly-tinted foundation and made up her eyes, a touch of blusher and lipstick, and it was 8:25 am.

"How's that," she said out loud.

Perfect timing – she had a last sip of the now almost cold tea.

"Here's to me," she whispered, a tight knot in her stomach, the sudden and only indication that today was the beginning of the greatest adventure to date.

Breakfast was in the dining room. A magnificent room was the only way to describe it, she told Harris and Peter later. Along with ten chairs around it in what looked like mahogany. A carpet that with even Claire's limited knowledge looked like Chinese silk in blues and creams with curtains at each of the picture windows of the exact cream but trimmed with the deepest of the blue and tie backs in the same blue. Frederick and Martine were already at the table, a crew member stood by a buffet table where cheeses, meats, scrambled eggs and fish stood on heated dishes.

As she entered the room, having been guided by a crew member who was waiting outside her door, Frederick rose to his feet.

"Ah, Miss Claire, perfect timing." Martine didn't look up from her plate, her long hair hanging over her face as to almost cover it.

"Good morning," Claire replied.

"Goodness, I've made it before Kostas," she laughed.

Frederick pulled a face. "Miss Claire, Mr Kostas always arrives after eight thirty. His guests are invited for 8:30, you understand?"

"Not really," replied Clare as she helped herself to scrambled egg and a delicious-looking croissant.

As she sat at the place indicated by Frederick opposite Martine, Kostas walked in. The atmosphere changed immediately, whatever it had been before was now charged with electricity. Martine looked up briefly and looked down again. Frederick jumped to attention. Only Claire sat smiling at him as she ate her first mouthful. He looked at her appraisingly, noting the clothes and how comfortably she wore them. They had been bought with great care from the Chanel boutique in Victoria. He was not unknown to them, but this time Frederick had been given very precise instructions, not the usual 'get something for her'.

As Kostas sat, the steward brought over a large portion of yoghurt on to which he poured honey until Kostas gave a brief nod. He took one spoonful then leaned back in his chair.

"Ah, that's better, Greek yoghurt, elixir of the gods." He laughed loudly, and they all smiled politely.

"Frederick, have you talked of our plans today?"

"I'm leaving," Martine said somewhat sullenly, Claire thought.

"I know, I know." Kostas sounded impatient when turning with a broad smile at Claire. "My dear, I was of course referring to 'our plans'."

"I have a dinner engagement this evening. I need to be home by 6 pm."

"What a shame. Nevertheless, we can have a bit of a sail and Frederick can show you around my floating domain."

Claire looked doubtful. As if sensing her doubts, Frederick added his voice to that of Kostas. "Really, Miss Claire, you need an hour to look around, then a nice lunch and back home for 6 o'clock. Surely you can manage that?"

"Of course," Claire made up her mind suddenly.

Enough of this prevaricating, this was what she had been planning for, hoping for, she would be mad to let this opportunity slip through her fingers.

Her made up dinner plans gave her the time 'let out' that she needed, and she would undoubtedly have dinner with Harris and Peter anyway as they so often did on a Sunday evening.

"Right," Kostas said, suddenly rising from the table as he spoke. "Frederick, you will see Martine off then show Claire around. I have some work to do. We will meet at 10 o'clock in the pool. Right?" He looked at Claire, even challenging her, she thought.

"Sounds wonderful," she replied brightly.

"You will find all you need for swimming in your cabin." Frederick, the ever- smooth man, said.

She couldn't help it; she was beginning to dislike him intensely.

"Well, goodbye, Martine," Claire held out her hand.

Martine looked up, disregarding once again the outstretched hand.

Claire noticed that she had dark circles under her eyes, and she looked as though she had been crying.

"I'll come to your cabin to say goodbye when I've collected my things. May I?" she added. A shade defensively, Claire thought.

"Of course, Martine, that would be lovely. I'll see you in a few minutes then."

She had noticed Frederick's frown and wondered what he could possibly object to in Martine coming to say goodbye, though Claire had to admit she was rather surprised. The girl had hardly spoken more than a few words to her, and now it seemed she wanted a cosy goodbye in the cabin. Perhaps, she was just anxious to see the cabin, Claire rationalised. She followed Kostas out of the dining salon and as he disappeared through the double doors of his suite, she arrived at her door.

The bed had already been made. Claire couldn't resist taking a peek. Her sheets were now of the palest blue, silk, of course. Fresh, new, softer than soft towels hung in the bathroom and noticing a drawer in the dressing table open, she glanced inside. The drawer had been opened for her benefit. Bikinis and bathing costumes were in neat sealed transparent packages. She had just lifted several out and put them on the bed to have a closer look when there was a knock on the door.

Martine stood there, small overnight bag in hand. "Can I come in?" Claire opened the door wider and Martine stepped inside and quickly closed the door behind her.

"I shouldn't have come. I don't really know why I have. But we're both girls, and girls have to stick together, don't they?"

Claire nodded, somewhat bemused.

"It's just that I thought you should know what kind of man he is." She read something in Claire's expression.

"It's not that I'm jealous of you, not really, that is. Well, perhaps a bit. You're so different from me, so sophisticated and everything."

Claire was beginning to feel a bit impatient. Where was all this leading?

"Well," she said helpfully. "It's just that he's a brute, Kostas. He is cruel, he likes to hurt, really hurt. I think secretly he prefers boys. When I first came here nearly a week ago now, there was this boy, couldn't have been more than 13. The first night," she hesitated. "The first night, Kostas made me watch him with the boy. It was horrible. He was crying out, but I couldn't understand, I think he was Greek or something."

Tears were welling from her eyes.

Her story was horrific, but was it true? Or was her jealously making her fabricate such a thing?

"Then he had me, the same way. I've never done that before. He hurt me. But then he gave me this."

She held out her wrist and Claire saw a bracelet that looked very familiar. "It sort-of helped. Then this past week…I can't tell

85

you things, I just can't. But once, he tied me to the bed, my hands and feet, and the crew came, four of them. Then Kostas said I was ready for him, but it wasn't him, it was a great big dildo thing. You know?"

Claire nodded.

She had never seen one, but she knew.

By now, Martine was sobbing. "I shouldn't have told you. He would kill me. He said he would if I ever spoke about anything on this ship. So please, don't tell him I told you, will you?" she pleaded.

Claire put her arms around the girl.

"I won't say anything, I promise."

She couldn't fail to believe at least parts of what she had heard.

However jealous Martine was, unless she was a superb actress, these tears were real. She fetched a dampened face cloth from the bathroom.

"Here, wipe your face. You don't want him to see you like this, do you?"

"He won't, he's working; it's that Frederick that will see me off. See, he has already given me this."

She took a fat envelope out of her bag. It had already been opened and Claire could see it was stuffed with $100 bills.

"I'll come and wave you off and thank you, Martine. Don't worry, I'll be careful."

The girls hugged and after one more wipe with the face cloth, they left the cabin.

Frederick was waiting at the top of the steps to the quay. At his side, Claire recognised the driver from last night.

As they drew close, Claire flashed a smile at Martine. Poor kid, only 18 and if only part of what she said is true, what an experience.

Frederick smiled as they drew close. "You two seem to have become friends all of a sudden?" he said.

Martine said nothing, so Claire filled the slightly awkward pause. "Martine's just been telling me what a lovely ship this is, and how she will miss it."

Frederick raised an eyebrow in obvious disbelief.

Damn, that didn't convince him at all, she thought.

"Georgios, take Miss Martine home. Make sure you take her all the way."

It seemed to Claire an odd thing to say. If he was taking her home, of course it would be all the way.

However, she squeezed Martine's arm and watched as the girl climbed into the back of the car where she had herself been only hours before.

Martine gave a brief wave and was gone. "If you will excuse me, Miss Claire, I shall be about ten minutes, then I can show you around, is that alright?"

"Fine," she responded, thinking it would give her time both to think over what Martine had said and also look at the swimwear and decide if she too wanted to jump ship now.

As she reached the cabin, she felt a slight movement and looking out, she saw they were already underway.

Too late to jump ship, she thought wryly.

Frederick made his way to Kostas' suite, going in through the double doors without knocking and from there through the private salon into the office. The hub of Kostas' empire.

Kostas looked up surprised. "Something the matter?" he said, noticing the expression.

"The microphone's paid off, Kostas. The girl talked."

"How much?"

"Pretty much everything."

"You've alerted Georgios?"

"She will never get home, and he will retrieve the goods, of course."

"Well done."

Without further comment, Kostas returned to the internet.

Frederick, not expecting thanks, but glad he had been able to serve Kostas yet again, left the salon and knocked on Claire's door.

The tour Frederick gave her of the yacht proved fascinating to Claire, albeit she did not see Kostas' suite, though Frederick mentioned it contained his personal salon, office and bedroom and bathrooms.

The main salon was a beautiful room, if slightly over opulent. Once, she would have revelled in the ornateness, now 'the new improved model', as she described herself to Harris and Peter at frequent intervals, had developed a better sense and taste and style, not unlinked to Peter's taste in clothes, make-up and hair and their taking her to various art galleries after Sunday's regular swim. Claire's swimming had caused Peter to have hysterics.

"You look like a duck," he had told her forthrightly, "holding your head out of the water like that."

"It's the only stroke I know," she had replied, slightly hurt. "And anyway, I don't want to get my hair wet. You only did it for me yesterday."

"Peter won't mind doing it again," Harris said in response. "Now, young Claire, we are going to teach you proper swimming. Aren't we, Peter?"

"If you say so, who am I to argue?" Harris smiled at Claire comfortingly. "Don't worry about your hair, darling. As I said, Peter will do it again!"

There was no way Claire would wriggle further.

So that first Sunday in the pool she had her first lesson in the crawl. She hated it, she almost hated Harris and Peter, but after the second lesson, she had begun to get the feel of it and by the third, she was proficient and, what was more, enjoying it too.

The tour continued, the gym, the guest's cabins, the three others apart from the one she was using. All identical in size though each with its own colour scheme.

Then down another gangway to the kitchen (galley, Frederick corrected her), the size of which surprised her. She had expected something fairly simple, even pokey, but like everything else on board, it was spacious and well laid out.

"Crew's quarters." Frederick waved his hand down a corridor.

"How many crew?" Claire wanted to know.

"Eight and the captain, nine with Georgios, who travels with us. We either hire a car, or as in Victoria, where we come regularly, Kostas keeps his own."

"If you would like to get changed now, Miss Claire, I think you will find Kostas waiting for you at the pool."

"I think you better show me the way, I might get lost!" Frederick smiled, "It does seem a little confusing at first with the different levels and gangways but you'll soon know it backwards."

"You expect me to come back then?"

"Of course, Miss Claire." Frederick spoke with a finality Claire found chilling, but he softened with a slight smile, which Claire noticed didn't seem to reach his eyes.

Once back in the cabin, she opened the various packs she had left strewn on the bed just prior to Martine's unexpected arrival, despite the fact that with her new modest bosom, she generally wore bikinis. She deliberately chose a simple navy and white one-piece.

She felt slightly sick and she was sure it was not the motion of the boat which was barely perceptible. It was being back in the room, remembering what Martine had said. Even if it was only partially true, it left her with an uncomfortable feeling and a slight disquiet at swimming with Kostas.

She collected the towelling robe she had noticed earlier hanging on the inside of the bathroom door and tied it round her. Barefooted, she left the room, heading in what she hoped was the right direction of the pool. Kostas was already there, looking remarkably lithe for such a big man as he swam up and down the pool. The windows had been opened and the freshness of the air made Claire shiver slightly. Pausing in his stroke, appraising her with a glance and noticing the shiver, Kostas called cheerily, "It's warmer in than out, I promise."

Blessing Harris and Peter for teaching her to swim properly, she executed a shallow dive and went straight into a stylish crawl.

"Are you good at everything you do, Claire?" Kostas called as she paused to look around at the end of her second length.

She smiled in response.

Kostas wouldn't have given her the time of day had he seen her when she first arrived in Canada.

They swam only up and down the pool, exchanging pleasantries. "Are you sure you can't stay on board for dinner?"

Amazingly, Claire detected a slightly begging tone and notched it up as a success point. She was making headway, real headway.

"No, Kostas, I can't, you know that, and I'm not prepared to let my friends down."

"Pity, we could have enjoyed a nice dinner à deux and really got to know each other."

"What, no Frederick?"

"There are times, my dear Claire, where even Frederick is excluded."

He sounded slightly annoyed and for a split second, Claire nearly weakened, but her inner resolve warned her this was not the time.

She swam to the end of the pool and climbed out and into the towelling robe. A steward came in with a tray.

"Hot chocolate or brandy?" Kostas called from the pool.

"Hmm, hot chocolate. What a lovely thought."

She sat back in one of the loungers as Kostas climbed out of the pool himself and pressed a switch on the wall. The windows closed and now the sunlight outside looked invitingly warm. The steward poured her a steaming cup of hot chocolate and a brandy, which he put down on the table between the loungers, giving himself time to collect Kostas' robe and help his master into it. Claire noticed no word of thanks, just a brief incline of the head.

"Ah, that's better," Kostas said, sinking back into the cushioned lounger and holding out his hand for the brandy which was handed to him immediately.

"Now, Claire, we are alone at last." The steward, taking the hint, left.

"Now, it is time you told me all about yourself."

"No, Kostas, I'd much rather learn about you. Where your home is, how long you stay on the yacht. So much more interesting, I'm sure."

She was lucky. Kostas enjoyed talking about himself, and she was able to postpone any 'history' she might decide appropriate to tell him when she was better prepared. Kostas talked of his home on the Island of Assos, where he was born, situated on the most beautiful island of Cephalonia in the southern Ionian Sea.

"From my village, from my house, I can see across the most beautiful small bay in the Ionian to where on a high hill are the remains of castle fortifications. Centuries ago, men started to build it as a fortification and still today as one walks amid the ruins one can close one's eyes and smell and taste the energy that still fills the place. Bold battles were fought over centuries and my little village is part of its history. Our bay, I've already said, is beautiful and agreeably small, so only one or two yachts can moor off bringing business to the restaurants but little tourism which is good."

"If it's so small," Claire said, "what happens when this…," she indicated the yacht, "when this arrives? How do you get into your lovely bay?"

"I don't," Kostas laughed. "We moor outside and the launch takes me in to the quayside."

Claire tried to imagine what it was like, but it was difficult never having been to Greece.

"It must be beautiful, I'd love to see it and climb up to the old castle."

"You will, Claire, I promise you, you shall. It is not many people who I take to my home, but you will be one of them."

Claire had spoken unthinkingly, it had all sounded so fascinating, now she had given him the idea that their 'friendship' was to grow.

A shiver struck her as thoughts of Martine crossed her mind.

What was she getting herself into?

Kostas noticed the shiver. "Time to get dressed, Claire. Lunch will be in half an hour. I shall see you there, and we can plan our afternoon. Perhaps, some fishing, huh?"

Claire got up and tightened the dressing gown around her.

Fishing! The thought of a fish on a hook had no appeal.

However, she smiled, not wanting to offend, and together they walked back towards the cabins. He left her at her door, kissing her lightly on the cheek before continuing down the corridor to his suite.

She sat on the bed, feeling a bit overwhelmed and a bit bemused yet again! Everything was working out as she had planned. It was almost too easy; yet, instead of the excitement she felt a certain coolness within her. Now was the time to pull back, if she was going to. Harris and Peter would certainly want her to, there was no way she could tell them the Martine story. She had already made her mind up earlier about that. At least she only had the afternoon to get through, fishing or no fishing.

Could she live with this man, she wondered? Could she sleep with him? If she agreed to marry him, if he asked her, that is, she would have to lay some ground rules to protect herself. There was no way she was prepared to be treated as Martine and presumably others before her had been treated. She had heard of pre-nuptial agreements and wondered if Kostas usually had that sort of legal arrangement with wives.

She got up suddenly from the bed and walked into the bathroom to take a shower. She thought she heard a sound and turned suddenly, but there was nothing. The hot water from the gold-leafed dolphins poured over her. She held her head and let the water cascade over her face. Kostas, watching her, courtesy of the lens fitted in every room including the bathroom, was enchanted. He felt himself grow hard and for a moment was tempted to go to her cabin, throw her on the bed and rape her. His willpower kept him where he was, putting his hand on his penis, he masturbated until he came, watching her intently as he did so. He leaned back in his chair and flicked off the camera, unbeknownst to her, he felt he had already taken her, though the thoughts of her warm flesh left him still wanting.

Several times during lunch, she found Kostas staring at her rather intently.

"You are putting me off my lunch, Kostas. Stop looking at me like that."

"Like what?" he replied innocently, glancing at Frederick who had joined them for lunch.

"I don't know," she answered defensively, "you are making me feel a little uncomfortable, that's all."

"Well, if that's all," Frederick said, "I wouldn't worry. Kostas is at his most charming today so don't try and change him."

Claire gasped, expecting Kostas to be angry, but he flashed Frederick a smile. 'Almost conspirational' was how she later described the look to Harris and Peter.

The fishing wasn't too bad. In fact, all Claire had to do was hold a rod for a while and when it started to pull, Kostas took over and played the large fish she had hooked until it could fight no longer. To see it flapping, still just alive, at her feet seemed very sad and she knew that she would never eat fish again without remembering the scene.

They were back at the dock, the space that Kostas paid a fortune for because of the size of the yacht. As she was about to climb down to the waiting car, Kostas handed her a tiny box.

"No presents, Kostas, I've already said."

"Then you will be breaking a tradition. Every female guest who spends some time aboard has a tiny souvenir of their visit. See?" He opened the box.

There was a fine gold chain, and as he lifted it up to show her, she saw a model of the yacht down to the port holes, which had tiny bits of blue glass in them which contrasted against the gold.

"It's a bauble, my dear Claire, and I would be most hurt if you decide not to accept it."

It was tiny, it was delightful.

Why not, if this was a tradition? It probably wasn't worth much more than a bouquet of flowers.

"Let me put it on for you. Turn around."

She dutifully turned, and he put it around her neck. She felt the warmth of his fingers as he fastened it. Putting her hand up, she touched the miniature yacht which nestled against her throat.

"Thank you, Kostas. I shall treasure it."

And she would, she decided, as the first of many gifts that she would utterly accept when the time was right, when her plans all came together.

Back in the flat, she telephoned Harris and Peter.

"I'm back, do come round this evening as usual, please. I've so much to tell you."

"You try and stop us," said Peter, who had answered the telephone. "I'll make the dinner. Pasta, okay?"

"Yum, you know I love your pasta dishes."

They agreed that 7 pm would be good and Claire went to hang her suit away and change out of Kostas' clothes. For some strange reason, she didn't want her friends to see her wearing something that Kostas had given her.

She left the golden yacht on though, noticing how the little blue stones sparkled back in the mirror. She looked at it more attentively, the 'portholes' had tiny white stones surrounding the blue.

So clever, she thought, never suspecting they were anything special. She put on a blouse and jeans, brushed her hair, put on some moisturiser and lipstick and had just had a final look in the mirror when her friends rang the doorbell.

Chapter 14

They wanted to know everything.

Peter was interested in décor and layout, Harris with the cuisine. He had heard from the chef at the restaurant that Kostas was an intolerant employer and one who given a less than perfect meal searched for a new chef. Harris said the correct one must be good as he had worked for Kostas for the past three years.

Claire realised that she hadn't paid due attention to the food, apart from breakfast which had been delicious, after that with thoughts of Martine on her mind she was watching and listening very carefully to everything Kostas and Frederick said to such an extent that she had eaten lunch without really noticing.

Harris was appalled. "Claire, how could you? Probably some of the finest food in the world and you didn't notice?"

He sat back in his chair and waved his fork at her in an admonitory way.

"Tell me, darling, what are you eating now?"

"Peter's delicious pasta, which I'm sure I'm enjoying more than I enjoyed lunch."

"Why, what happened?" Peter leaned forward, his eyes meeting her in a concerned way.

Claire started, then had to bite her tongue to stop herself telling all. If they knew about Martine, they would try everything they could to stop her further involvement.

"I had to be so much on guard," she said speaking slowly. "Kostas wanted to know all about me and I hadn't worked everything out, you know, Lenny, the adoption, my marriage."

They nodded in unison.

"Anyway, fortunately, I managed to turn the tables and get him talking about himself and his home. It was quite interesting actually."

"What's that you are wearing? I don't think I've seen it before." Harris asked curiously.

Claire's hand flew to her throat.

"This?" she said in a nonchalant tone as possible. "Kostas gave it to me. Apparently its worth next to nothing and every female visitor to The Pandora receives one as a memento of their visit."

"Claire!" The two men spoke as one.

Harris continued "I thought you weren't going to accept anything?"

"I sent the bracelet back." Claire's tone was defensive. "This is only a very little thing, and he acted really offended when I tried to refuse it."

"May I, Claire?" Peter held out his hand. She undid the fastener and handed it to him.

"Peter knows a great deal about jewellery," Harris said. "What do you think, Peter?" he continued.

"Bauble it may be to Kostas, but the little blue stones are dots of sapphire and surrounding the 'port holes' are the most perfectly matched minute seed pearls."

"You are so bloody knowledgeable, Peter. Really, I love you both dearly but you are like a pair of mother hens, fussing over me."

Peter silently handed the necklace back. She couldn't bring herself to put it on. Her friends were cross with her and she didn't need that now. She wanted support, not haranguing.

"Subject dropped," Harris said.

He had noticed Claire's distress, enough was enough; they had made their position clear. He glanced across the table and Peter gave an imperceptible nod as if reading his mind. The mood lightened as they talked of other things.

That night, as she lay in bed, Claire let her mind drift over the last 24 hours. So much had happened, including a step forward in her relationship with Kostas.

She sensed intuitively that Kostas would make his move soon, and she must be prepared. She must also prepare her semi-fictitious background, excluding her marriage to Len and her son Lenny.

No, on second thoughts, she was no virgin, so decided she would tell him of a tragic marriage and the death of a much-loved husband.

She tidied up a few details in her mind, then with a sigh of relief settled down to sleep, her mind full of glorious times in the future on The Pandora and all thoughts of Martine put firmly in a box in her mind labelled 'do not open'.

The first flowers were delivered before she left for the restaurant. Ten white lilies whose scent filled the flat overpoweringly.

The note accompanying them said merely, *I enjoyed your company.*

He didn't eat at the restaurant that evening and Claire couldn't make up her mind whether she was relieved or disappointed.

The next morning, more flowers.

She had had to throw the lilies out. It seemed a terrible waste, but their perfume was cloying and overpowering in such a relatively small space.

This time, fortunately, it was roses, white. He obviously liked white flowers.

The note read: *Breakfast tomorrow, Wednesday, on Pandora before you leave for the restaurant. Georgios will collect you at 8 am. K.*

He just assumed she would go, just like that. She wondered whether to send him a note back saying: *Sorry, inconvenient*, but had to remind herself she wanted the relationship to progress, now was no time for stalling!

That morning, she telephoned Hugo. She had been worrying for some time about the flat. At any time, Hugo could fail to renew the lease.

She loved the flat. It was her first real home, a home that she had created with a certain amount of help from Harris and Peter, of course.

Hugo was affable. Presuming Claire had telephoned to ask after Lenny, he chatted for several minutes about the boy's progress, his friends, his enjoying ice hockey and sailing. Claire listened politely. It was like listening to any over-fond parent talking about their son. Her relationship with Lenny was, as far as she was concerned, now totally non-existent, at the best of times, its existence had been muted.

Finally, he stopped droning on about Lenny and asked if there was anything she wanted or needed.

"Actually," Claire said, feeling suddenly a bit afraid. Perhaps, she should let sleeping dogs lie.

"It's about the flat, Hugo."

"Oh, I forgot to send you the deeds."

"I beg your pardon?" she said, not being quite sure what he had said or meant.

"I've had the flat put in your name, Claire. It's yours."

Claire was stunned. Her flat, her very own flat, and she had been about to talk about a mortgage and payments to purchase it from him.

"I can't," she protested feebly. "I can't just take it just like that, Hugo!"

"Claire, you have made our lives worth living again. Ellie and I are truly happy after all the grief. Your generosity in letting us adopt Lenny is nothing compared with the flat."

"Does Ellie know?"

"She knows that I found a flat for you. I never told her the circumstances, and she doesn't need to know, does she?"

There was a definitely nervous question there, she thought. Well, she would accept it. Why not? Some niggle at the back of her mind told her it was 'payment for Lenny'.

So what? He was happy, they were happy and she had her own bit of real estate. She was a woman of property!

"I'll put the deeds in the post." Hugo interrupted her musings. "I suggest you lodge them with your lawyer."

"Right. Well, thank you, Hugo," she said a little belatedly. "Thank you very much."

He murmured goodbye. She, then having put down the telephone, danced around the room.

"It's mine, all mine."

Everything suddenly looked even more special than before. She touched the back of the sofa as she danced round it. Picked up a cushion and threw it joyfully into the air. The doorbell interrupted her in full flow. She glanced at her watch. It was, of course, precisely 8:00 am.

Chapter 15

It was Georgios, as smartly turned out as ever.

"Good morning, Miss Claire, the car is downstairs."

Claire felt an impish desire to pretend disappointment that he hadn't brought it with him, but decided against it. Just because she felt bubbly about the flat, he wouldn't understand her silliness!

She hoped to tell Harris about it when she arrived at the restaurant later, but for now she must marshal her thoughts and calm down, ready to breakfast with Kostas and try and discover what his next move would be.

Promptly at 8:30 am, she was once again in the dining salon, her scrambled eggs and bacon smelt delicious, but she knew better than to begin without the man himself.

He walked in, interrupting her chain of thought.

"Ah, Claire, my dear, all dressed for work, I see."

She was indeed in one of her simple black suits, today the one with the deep turquoise cuff and collar revers.

She nodded briefly and picked up her fork.

Frederick pulled a chair out for himself and, Claire could tell, was somewhat piqued when Kostas with an impetuous wave of his hand said, "Frederick, would you please eat elsewhere today."

He obviously didn't expect Frederick to demur and immediately turned back to Claire. Claire, however, saw the thunderstruck look on Frederick's face, and she felt an unreserved moment of pleasure. He really was such a servile bore, always hanging around, and he was also, she had decided, rather creepy in his ever obsequious way.

Having finished his yoghurt and honey, Kostas sat back in his chair and put his hands together, fingers spread. She was to learn this was a regular pose when he had something important to say, for now, though, she looked at him and smiled. Here she was having breakfast aboard the beautiful Pandora and Kostas seemed less daunting by the minute. The Martine saga was firmly locked away in her mind, and she had thrown away the key!

For a while, they talked in a desultory way. She used the opportunity to talk briefly of her marriage. He listened but she felt he was not fully attentive. Finally, he stopped her mid-stream and looked at her steadily.

"Claire, will you give up your work and sail with me on The Pandora? I will give you a good life, even take you to my beautiful Assos."

Claire's heart missed a beat.

Then she realised he was not asking her to marry him. She was being asked to become his mistress. It was only one notch up from the bimbos he usually had in tow.

For a moment, she was tempted. The old Claire would have been, but the new, wiser Harris and Peter trained Claire knew exactly what to do.

She stood up and picked up her handbag. Her tone was cold – her eyes she hoped looked a mixture of sad and angry.

"How could you believe I would want to become your mistress," she said.

She saw his eyebrows shoot up, the fingers of his hands tapped together. "I thought you realised that was my idea," his tone was placatory, patient even, as if he was talking to someone who hadn't quite grasped the concept of what he was offering. "You will have everything, anything you want, here, in my flat in New York, my house in France and Assos. What more could any woman want?"

"Marriage," she replied simply, and without a backwards glance, she walked out of the salon. The wretched Frederick was hovering – obviously hadn't wanted to miss a thing, probably hadn't eaten any breakfast in order to be there now.

"Are you leaving, Miss Claire, already?"

"Yes," she said nodding briefly, her heart still racing at the enormity of what she had done.

"I'll tell Georgios to bring the car."

"Don't bother," she replied. "I prefer to walk."

She, of course, arrived at the restaurant way ahead of time. Using her staff key, she let herself in and knowing Michael would be in his office, headed in that direction. He looked up as she stood in the open doorway. God, she looked attractive: her cheeks were flushed; she seemed to be breathing faster than normal. If he wasn't a happily married man, he could have fancied her at that moment.

Something in her expression stopped his fantasies. He didn't have to ask.

She just blurted it out. "I've probably lost you a valuable customer, Michael. I've just refused to become Kostas' mistress."

There, she'd said it.

Mentally, she repeated it to herself again. She must be mad, she should have agreed.

"Well done, Claire, you would have disappointed me if you'd agreed. So what, we lose Kostas. There are others, plenty of others."

Kostas did not come to the restaurant that evening. Claire half dreaded, half wanted him to appear. Finally the day, the long day was over, she longed to be back in the comfort and security of her own flat.

She smelt the flowers before she saw them. Lilies, white lilies, their cloying perfume filling the corridor. She automatically picked up the bouquet and put her key in the lock – once inside, she dropped the flowers on the coffee table, unsure how to deal with their perfume, which was once again overpowering her.

The note in the small envelope pinned to the wrapping demanded to be read.

Will you forgive me? K.

She felt a moment of triumph, quickly followed by despair, he asked for forgiveness. Hardly the same as asking her to marry him. She picked up the flowers and walked determinedly into the kitchen, lifting the lid of the rubbish chute she pushed them in and down.

By the time she went to bed, the perfume had almost faded, but still lingering in the air the reminder that Kostas was playing his games.

By the next morning, she had calmed down and could see the funny side of her actions of the previous evening. Once again, she prepared herself for work, wondering what, if anything, the day would bring.

Thankfully, for a second evening Kostas did not appear in the restaurant but when she left at 11:30, Georgios was outside standing by the limo.

"Ah, Miss Claire. Kostas asked me to drive you home."

"Thank you, Georgios, but it's such a short distance, and I prefer to walk."

He didn't argue, just touched his head in a half salute and drove off. The night air refreshed her, and she arrived home feeling tired and, for some unaccountable reason, depressed. Tonight, no cloying smell of lilies; instead, as she drew nearer to her front door, the delicate smell of roses greeted her.

The perfume was at least acceptable, she thought, *but what now?*

Once indoors, she tore the envelope off the wrapper and opened it.

This time he wrote.

May we talk? I will be in the restaurant tomorrow. K.

'May', he actually wrote 'may', no demand, but a slightly, humble, would be too strong a word, but it was not the usual demanding tone that he so often used to bully his way.

Thoughtfully, she put the flowers in her one and only vase. The redness of the roses seemed stark against the white of her sofa and chair.

Still holding the note, she undressed and went to bed, propping the note against her clock radio, wondering what next.

She dreamt that night that she was sitting in the dining salon – the room was much larger than in real life though and the table much longer.

Kostas, in her dream, sat in his usual place at the head of the table, whilst she was wearing a tiara in her hair and a necklace around her neck, the diamonds and rubies the size of bantam eggs, her head feeling pulled down by their weight. She tried to raise her hand to eat but the weight of jewels around her wrist held it down and as course after course was served, she could only look and smell the delicious food, but was unable to eat.

She spoke to Kostas, but she knew he was too far away to hear.

In her dream, she knew loneliness she had never felt before and she could feel the tears pouring silently from her eyes.

She woke suddenly, her whole body bathed in perspiration. She could almost feel the weight of the jewellery and it was with relief that she sat up in bed and put on the bedside lamp.

Kostas' note, its heavy black writing on the white card, seemed to mock her.

Reaching for it, she tore it in two and threw it on the floor. Climbing out of bed, she went to the kitchen and poured herself a glass of orange juice.

What was happening to her? What power had this man over her that he came into her dreams?

For the first time, she seriously considered turning her back on him and having decided that would probably be the best course of action. She settled back in bed and slept peacefully for the balance of the night.

The next morning, Michael informed her that Kostas had booked his usual table. "I thought", said the over considerate Michael, "that you might prefer it if Henry looked after him, and you did one of his tables."

"How right you are," she said, relieved.

The thought of serving Kostas tonight was much too uncomfortable.

"You are very good to me, Michael," she said heart.

He smiled and patted her gently on the shoulder. "You've been good to me, good for business too. The least I can do is take care of my staff."

The evening arrived all too quickly. When Kostas arrived, he managed to attract her attention just by his presence. Their eyes met. He looked stern, she thought, smiling very briefly before moving on to care for a customer's needs.

If Kostas was annoyed not to be served by Claire, he didn't show it. Indeed, he behaved impeccably. For once, he was alone. He ate slowly, as if deliberately putting off the moment when he would finish his dinner.

Finally, when most of the customers had left, he asked Michael to join him for a brandy. Then without even a glance in Claire's direction, he left the restaurant. Twenty minutes later, Claire said her goodnights and let herself out into the night.

Once again, the limo was there.

Once again, Georgios gave her his half salute.

This time, however, the interior of the car was lit and Kostas sat puffing on the inevitable cigar.

"Mr Papadofulas would like to speak with you," Georgios said, opening the rear door as he spoke.

She hesitated for a moment and Kostas, sensing this, leaned forward and in his most charming manner said, "I think you would like to give me some time, Claire, when you hear what I have to say."

Without a word, she stepped in and the door closed silently behind her.

Georgios, obviously primed, drove the short distance to her flat.

"May I come up?"

Again the 'may' word.

"Why not?" she replied.

What had she to lose?

They were silent as they went up in the lift. Claire usually ran up the stairs, but in deference to his weight, decided to advocate the lift.

He looked around appraisingly, smiling when he saw the roses. "Unlike the lilies which you threw out," he said softly.

Claire was taken aback. How had he found out? Probably bribed the concierge, she thought crossly, and correctly, as it happened.

He sat down unasked, on one of the white armchairs; deliberately she sat on the other.

"Claire," he began speaking slowly and clearly. "You have provided me with a dilemma."

She raised her eyebrows by way of response.

"After the marriages I have had, I decided never again. I was prepared to make you my mistress. Indeed wife in all but name. But no, independent woman that you are, that would not do. I admire principles in other people, anyway." He chuckled at his own joke.

"So, what to do?" He looked at her questioningly. She met his gaze and said nothing. This was getting really interesting. Had she dared, she hoped that she pulled it off.

"So, Claire, I have decided I will marry you."

No romantic proposal this, no asking her whether she would like to become the fourth Mrs K. Still, now was no time to nit-pick. It was now or never.

Trying hard to keep any tremor out of her voice and to still her quaking knees, she answered in as calm a voice as possible. "Thank you, Kostas, I would be delighted to marry you."

It was, she thought, *as if a business deal had been concluded*. He stood up suddenly.

"On The Pandora, next Sunday, 6 pm."

"Do I have any choice?" she said laughingly, trying to lighten the somewhat tense atmosphere.

"No," he answered shortly. "Frederick will see you tomorrow to discuss arrangements. Goodnight, Claire."

He stood up, and she followed suit. He stepped towards her, and she prepared herself for a passionate kiss. She felt his lips brush her cheek and opened her eyes in surprise. That was it! For a moment, she felt defrauded then her sense of humour got the better of her. She responded in kind, kissing him lightly on his cheek. He smelt of cigars and aftershave.

He walked to the door; she stood still, rooted to the spot.

"Goodnight," he said again, letting himself out.

Her legs gave way under her, she sank down in the chair she had vacated only moments earlier and found that she was crying. Not silent tears, but great gulping sobs. Once she had hoped she would not only find a rich husband, but romantic fool that she

106

was, she had even hoped for love. Once again, love eluded her. She was to be trapped in a loveless marriage.

Then the cool, calm fortune huntress started to rationalise. She would be rich; RICH – she would live in style – a style that she would enjoy. She would have endless supplies of beautiful clothes and jewels. Momentarily, her dream of being weighed down with jewels came into her mind, but she dismissed it as the nonsense it was. She was going to be Mrs Papadofulas, married to one of the richest men in the world.

Could she have even dreamed she would 'pull it off'?

"Clever Claire," she murmured to herself, looking at her watch as she did.

She would love to ring Harris and Peter but they would be in bed by now, her news would have to wait until morning.

Of course, she watched the clock all night, trying desperately to sleep, her over-active mind fantasised about her future. Her future as Mrs P. She pictured herself lolling around, being waited on, pictures of handsome young men paying court to her. She imagined walking into couture houses, ordering vast quantities of superlative clothes. The one thing she didn't fantasise was of her future with Kostas. She couldn't, didn't want to imagine his love-making, although she sensed already that she would be unmoved.

By the time morning eventually arrived, she was emotionally and physically exhausted.

For the first time ever, she dragged herself to the restaurant, but once there, the excitement made her forget her weariness. It was, of course, Harris that she went to first. She told him word for word what had happened the previous evening when she left the restaurant. She could tell from his face that he had mixed emotions, though as he hugged her and wished her well, he didn't voice the concerns she had registered on his face.

Michael was delighted. Though he told her that the restaurant would not be the same without her, she had really carved herself a special niche.

Peter arrived at seven that evening. Harris had phoned him, and he was already excited at the prospect of helping Claire choose her gown, doing her hair and putting together a trousseau.

His excitement was infectious and for the first time, Claire herself began to feel the excitement taking over, her calm resolve disappeared. She became like any other bride, nervous, excited and not a little daunted.

With only four days to prepare, Michael wanted her to leave that evening, but she insisted she would work for two more days, for she felt sure with Peter's help she would manage all she needed to in that time.

Of Kostas, there was no sign, but Frederick appeared and reappeared at regular intervals. It was he who arrived at her flat with the engagement ring. The hugest diamond Claire had ever seen. It was a little loose so Frederick took it away to have it corrected. Flowers arrived from Kostas, with a note saying that Frederick would explain about shopping. Claire waited for Frederick to appear again. He soon returned after a few hours with the ring, now a snug fit. He also had a list of shops (all the best ones on Vancouver Island) where Kostas had accounts.

"Anything you choose, just charge to his account," Frederick explained. "Except jewellery, he likes to choose that himself."

The last two days were a panic. The wedding group was to be small. Harris, Peter and Michael, his wife, being Claire's only guests. She would have liked to invite Ellie, Hugo and Lenny but with Kostas not knowing the truth of her past, she felt she had no option but to exclude them as one of the trio might let something slip.

Frederick was to be Kostas' 'best man' and the crew would make up the remaining guest list.

Peter was brilliant as only Peter could be. He took Claire to one of his favourite boutiques and helped her choose a simple but stunning outfit. She didn't feel she could be too bridal, but she wanted to look like a bride.

The outfit was of the palest rose, a simple short sleeved princess style dress, with matching coat. The hat was perhaps the pièce de résistance – the same rose but with a cloudy white flower covering the crown, the wide brim slightly piped up.

"So as not to hide your face," Peter remarked.

He found shoes that toned and a small neat handbag.

"Not that you will need it for the wedding, but great to have when you wear the outfit again, that is," he added half seriously, "if once you are the wealthy Mrs P, you will ever wear anything more than once."

Claire was in fact never to wear the ensemble again.

Sunday morning dawned bright and crisp. Peter and Harris arrived at the flat at 7:30 am. They seemed more excited now than she was. Suddenly, for no reason, she felt nothing – a sort of emptiness. She rationalised that it was because she was turning her back on a period of her life that had been the happiest she had ever been. She had grown to respect herself, had made true friends, she knew Lenny was safe and happy and now she felt as if she was on the edge of a volcano about to fall into its molten depths. In despair, she confided her emotions, or lack of them, to her friends. Harris looked worried for a moment – but Peter brushed her words aside with 'bride's nerves'. He was enjoying himself far too much to be put off.

Harris pulled himself together and hugged the bride to be. "He's right, darling Claire."

Reassured, Claire let herself be made up and hair coiffed by the ever- talented Peter. Harris helped her into her dress. Peter adjusted the hat. They stood back to admire their handiwork.

"You look stunning," Peter declared and Harris, for once lost for words, could only nod and smile in agreement.

The doorbell made them all start. Frederick stood there smiling (*his somewhat irritating smile*, Claire thought inwardly). She really couldn't bring herself to like him.

"You look excellent," he said crisply. "Georgios is below with the car."

Claire took one final look at her flat.

"You will take care of it for me?" she said to her friends in a whisper.

They nodded. They were glad she was keeping it, a part of her would always remain in Victoria and if she ever needed it, she would have a home to return to.

Chapter 16

The aft deck had been decorated with flowers linked from halyard to halyard creating a flower bower to the ceremony.

A local minister had been engaged for the ceremony, negotiated after a generous donation had been made to his church. Kostas, wearing a white suit and blue shirt with a navy tie, managed to look quite elegant despite his bulk and stocky build. Claire's heart fluttered with nervous anticipation as her eyes took in the scene.

Kostas stepped forward and took her by the arm. "You look very beautiful, Claire," she smiled at his look of approval and her spirits lifted. It was going to be alright after all.

The trio of musicians hired for the occasion played the Mendelsohn Bridal March. The minister cleared his throat as the couple stood in front of him and the music ceased. The words came and went. Claire heard a voice and knew it was hers but it seemed removed from her somehow.

Then Peter, Harris and Michael were kissing her and champagne was flowing. There was laughter and Claire felt happy, really happy. Her friends were happy, she could see it on their faces, a warm glow seemed to surround her. Perhaps, it was only the champagne, but Kostas looked positively benign – his expression seemed softer, kinder, even Frederick seemed less irritating now as if only her over active imagination had made her feel uncomfortable about him.

"It's midnight," Harris finally whispered in her ear. "Time all good guests should leave the bride and groom." Peter, Michael and Helen, his wife, followed suit, wishing her happiness and shaking Kostas by the hand before going ashore.

Claire, with Kostas by her side, and Frederick (*as ever*, her mind said) hovering nearby, watched their guests leave, calling goodnights.

Harris and Peter blew her extravagant kisses, which Claire returned enthusiastically, enjoying the mood that seemed to be all persuading.

Suddenly, they were gone, the night beyond the yacht silent, only faint sounds from the shore, indicating they were still moored alongside the quay.

Kostas interrupted her thoughts, suggesting a final nightcap. She walked slowly ahead of him to the now deserted aft deck. The flowers moved forlornly in the breeze, the chairs, where the musicians had sat, now empty. Frederick appeared with two brandies.

"Anything else, Kostas?" he enquired.

A brief shake of the head.

"Goodnight, Madam." Frederick gave a half bow which Claire felt mocking and then chided herself. Why must she always think the worst of Frederick? But she couldn't help herself.

Kostas finished his brandy. Claire put her glass down, having only touched the fiery liquid to her lips.

"Time for bed, I think," Kostas smiled agreeably. Claire nodded, unable to think of any reason to postpone the moment.

Together they walked down into the salon and from there down the corridor to the two double doors at the far end. The room she had never seen before.

Kostas threw open the doors and led her inside. It was a second salon, but if the first was luxurious this was fabulous. A silk Chinese carpet in red and cream covered the floor. Louis Quinze furniture, which she subsequently learned was genuine, was placed carefully and attractively. A large round table with an arrangement of white roses almost took Claire's breath away, red damask curtains reached from ceiling to floor, trimmed and tied back with ties of cream damask matching the cream in the carpet. The walls were covered with pictures, many of which seemed familiar to Claire although she at that time did not realise that these were all originals. She recognised several Monets, a Degas and even a small blue period Picasso.

Leading her by the hand, Kostas opened a door that she hadn't noticed as it was covered in the same fabric as the walls and had been designed to be unnoticed except by those with particularly observant eyes. It led into the bedroom. A magnificent four poster was the dominant feature. "Your dressing room and bathroom," Kostas said opening a door to his left.

"Where is yours?" Claire's voice was bemused; she had not expected quite such grandeur.

"Adjacent," he replied, waving in the general direction, enjoying watching her expression as she marvelled at the luxurious beauty.

He liked nothing better than an appreciative audience.

"I shall shower," he said somewhat abruptly and disappeared into his dressing room. One of the nightdresses and negligees that had been chosen with such care lay on the bed.

Picking it up, she walked towards her own dressing room to undress and shower. Feeling somewhat shy, she returned to the bedroom to find Kostas already there. He sat in one of the chairs by the picture window, looking out into the darkness, apparently deep in thought.

When she walked in, he looked up and smiled appreciatively. She did look lovely. Her hair gleamed. Her face, clear of any makeup, glowed, her figure beneath her flimsy robes provided a tantalising outline. He felt enthusiasm rising and held out his hand, indicating that he wanted her to walk over to him. She stood in front of him, feeling the colour flooding her face. She couldn't believe how shy she felt. The last time she had made love had been with Hugo (on his yacht – a somewhat smaller yacht, a voice inside her mocked).

Kostas stood suddenly. He eased the negligee and nightgown from her and indicated the bed.

Their lovemaking was, Claire thought afterwards, *predictable. Whatever Kostas might think, he was not the world's greatest lover.*

112

Claire gave her all, but once again, she felt a sense of disappointment. First Len, who was the world's most boring lover. Hugo was, well, he was Ellie's and it had been momentary madness.

Kostas, though, seemed to be making love as if he was doing it according to certain written rules.

His kisses, seemingly passionate, were dry and hard. He touched her breasts and the rest of her body lingeringly. Claire felt he was trying to be gentle.

She became aroused despite him, longing for love, longing to be loved, all her sexual passions flooded her being, and she responded to his every touch.

Then it was over. For a while he held her, then when he thought she was asleep, he carefully eased himself away and moved silently across the cabin, into his dressing room and into his bathroom.

For a while, Claire waited, expecting any moment that he would return, but gradually her eyes grew heavy, and she finally drifted off to sleep.

She woke suddenly and for a moment was disoriented. She put out her arm feeling for Kostas. The place beside her was empty, the sheets cold. He had not, she realised, returned to her side. Something had woken her; she tried to think what sound had disturbed her, then she heard it again and knew it was the same sound, the sound of a child crying.

Sitting bolt upright in bed, she listened intently. It could not be a child. No one on board, none of the crew had a wife and child with them, it was a totally masculine crew, yet it sounded; it was the sound of a child in distress.

Unhesitatingly, she got out of bed and pulling her negligee around her, its delicateness hardly providing cover, but modesty was not uppermost in her mind. She pressed the door handle down, her mind racing ahead. She would search the yacht and find that sobbing child. The door would not open, she smiled, wryly thinking for once something was not perfect, a stuck door, then as she tried it again, she realised it was not stuck, it was locked. The realisation that she was locked in hit her like a body blow. Anger took over from frustration. How dare he? How could he?

She walked towards his dressing room, assuming he was in there. The room was empty, the bathroom door ajar, she peered cautiously around. That room too was empty. Then she noticed the door at the far side, she turned the handle; that too was locked. This was crazy!

She quickly returned through her own dressing room to her bathroom, had she seen a door there but perhaps just hadn't noticed? There was no door, she was locked in and couldn't pursue the sound she had heard. She listened intently, the only sound was the gentle purring of the engines, the motion so slight that she hadn't realised they pulled away from the quayside.

Not knowing what to do next, she sat on the side of the bed. Her wedding night, locked into her cabin, her new husband somewhere, but certainly not by her side. Her watch showed 3:45am. The phone, of course! She picked it up and then dropped it quickly. How could she inform a member of the crew that she was locked in her cabin? With a furious sound, she lay down on the bed, willing the morning to arrive.

To her surprise, she must have slept, she felt movement at her side.

Kostas leaned over her. "Awake then, my little bride."

He thought she had slept all night. He didn't realise that she was awake.

He had been gone from her side for several hours.

"Kostas, why was the cabin door locked?"

For the first time ever, she had taken him off-guard.

He looked startled.

"Locked?" he repeated, slightly defensively, she thought.

"I heard something, a child crying. I tried the door and the one from your bathroom. Where does that lead to, by the way?"

"Oh, I'm a restless sleeper. I didn't want to disturb you so I slept for part of the night in the other bedroom."

He hadn't, she noticed, answered the question about the crying child.

"I heard a child," she repeated. "It sounded distressed."

To her surprise, he burst out laughing.

"The seagulls," he said. "Lots of people make the same mistake."

Claire looked unconvinced.

"It sounded so much like a child," but her voice wavered.

Could it have just been the wheeling and calling of the gulls? In the night, in a strange place, had her mind played tricks on her?

"I must have been mistaken," she said slowly.

Yet, something deep within her was not convinced.

Had she overheard the conversation that took place later between Kostas and Frederick she would have been horrified. Meantime, Kostas patiently explained about the locked bedroom door. "Frederick automatically locks it at night as I tend to come and go through my other door. I will see that it does not happen again. As for the other door," he continued, "you must be mistaken. The handle is stiff, I admit. I will have that seen to as well."

He then stroked her body, bringing her quickly to orgasm but made no attempt to satisfy himself.

When she demurred, he smiled gently down at her.

"I am an old man, my dear Claire, once every 24 hours is all I can manage. I hope you will forgive me."

She nodded, feeling slightly uncomfortable, but not quite sure why.

He used the phone and ordered fresh orange juice and coffee. When it arrived, he excused himself, saying he must deal with some urgent business, but would see her at breakfast.

"It must never happen again," Kostas told Frederick. "She heard. It woke her. Keep his mouth taped at <u>all</u> times except when he is eating and make sure he is quiet while he does that. Just a few more times and it will be the end."

Frederick nodded.

"The bedroom door," he enquired, "unlocked but when we have company, see to it that she has something in her last drink."

Again, Frederick nodded, unperturbed by his master's request. He liked the thought that the bitch was to be controlled, it appeared to his baser nature.

Chapter 17

Lazy day followed lazy day as they sailed towards their first destination, which Kostas told his bride was to be San Francisco.

Claire was thrilled, she had seen San Francisco so many times on film and now she was to see for herself the street cars and hilly street crossing hilly street!

Shopping would be fun. She needed more swimwear and casual clothes. Although she dressed for dinner each evening, her days were spent in a bikini or if it was a tad chilly, in linen trousers and a light top – she just needed more variety and Kostas seemed to enjoy her spending his money.

He had already given her a stunning diamond and emerald necklace as a wedding present and as he fastened it around her throat the first time, the image of her dream flashed into her mind.

"Why do you smile, Claire?" Kostas had wanted to know.

He laughed when he heard about the dream.

"I've never heard a woman complain about too much jewellery." His tone was dry. "Would you rather I sent them back?" He ran his fingers under the necklace at her throat.

She shivered slightly for some reason.

"No, Kostas. I love it." She spoke, quickly embarrassed that she had shivered under his touch.

A few days later, on her way to her cabin, she met Thoma, one of the crew. He was carrying a tray on which rested a half-filled glass of milk and a banana skin – one small empty plate indicated that the food had been on the tray at some stage.

"Why, Thoma, where have you come from?" She spoke in English, her Greek still very limited, though she was trying very hard.

The one thing, perhaps the only thing Frederick was good at, she sometimes thought. He was a good teacher. Thoma answered hesitatingly. She felt he looked uncomfortable and thought perhaps her tiny bikini was the cause.

He mumbled something – someone ill, she thought he said. Later in her cabin, she was puzzled who down their corridor could have been ill. No crew on this level and the corridor only led to their quarters.

At dinner that night, she asked Kostas. For a split second, she felt she had caught him unawares – but then as smooth as ever his answer made her cross that he had even enquired.

"My dear Claire, what an inquisitive soul you are. One of the crew."

"In our corridor?" she interrupted.

"No, my dear, Thoma had no doubt been on the way back from our sick crewman when Frederick asked him to check with me. We were both concerned and I had asked Thoma to report to me on how he was."

"Who?" Claire was still curious.

"Stephen," Kostas answered smoothly. "Satisfied, my dear?" He sounded calm, but Claire could sense an edge in his voice.

"Of course," quickly, she changed the subject, determined to find out for herself how Stephen was.

Claire was sleeping heavily these days, more heavily than she could ever remember. Sometimes she was asleep before Kostas came to bed and in the morning when she woke he would smile reproachfully.

"My little bride, asleep again when I come to bed," he would say.

Try as she might, her eyelids grew heavy and in the mornings she felt heavy and lethargic – she wondered if she was ill. They were making good time, the captain told her one day, two more days and they would be arriving in San Francisco.

At breakfast, unusually, Frederick spoke in Greek. Claire thought he said the cargo had gone.

"What cargo?" she asked innocently. Kostas' eyebrows shot upwards and Frederick looked taken aback.

Kostas laughed. "My dear Claire, Frederick tells me your Greek is really coming on, but you misunderstood then, he was talking about our supplies, one of my favourite wines, unfortunately, Frederick had under ordered. Very unusual, Frederick, I must say, this must not happen again."

"It will not, rest assured." Frederick looked distinctly uncomfortable.

Later, Claire looked up the word she had heard; *gomos,* in Greek it was cargo. He had said cargo.

Nevertheless, she wondered if perhaps there was a similar word that she had mistakenly translated as 'cargo' so she spent some time checking similar sounding words, even going over what Kostas had said Frederick had said, word by word. It just didn't make sense. He had said cargo.

Mysteries continued. She had sought out Stephen and in a carefully thought out phrase had asked him if he was better. She had said, "Are you better, Stephen?"

Stephen had answered in Greek "I have not been ill, Madam."

How she wished she could get to the bottom of this. She felt it just didn't make sense at times. At least she had started to feel better, but she had gone from one extreme to the other – now she lay awake unable to sleep. Kostas stayed by her side now night after night and she tried hard not to disturb him, lying as still as she could. But one night, he became aware of restlessness.

"My dear Claire, whatever is the matter?"

She confided that she just couldn't seem to sleep. "Probably I'm too excited about arriving in San Francisco," she said.

"Would you like a mild sedative? I always keep them handy for myself."

"No, thank you," she replied firmly, "I don't like taking anything unless I really need to, but I'm sorry if I am disturbing you."

After three or four nights, she found she was sleeping better again, though thankfully not the very deep sleep of the recent past and the early morning lethargy had totally disappeared. She rose early and swam and felt better than she had since almost the first day of her marriage. Kostas seemed delighted at the change in her and was considerably more attentive than he had been of late.

Their arrival at San Francisco was all that she could have hoped for. The crew too seemed to be looking forward to their arrival. The whole atmosphere on board seemed to have lightened. She would never forget her first sight of the harbour at San Francisco. It was dusk, the lights blazed from the shore; it looked like fairyland to Claire as she stood on deck, leaning against that rail.

Kostas stood beside her.

"The first time for anything is always the best," he murmured in her ear. "Like the first time I saw you, the first time we made love, the first kiss, eh, Claire, do you agree?"

She nodded, letting her mind drift to the first uninspired kiss, the first lovemaking.

In her opinion, the first time for anything was probably the most disappointing but she certainly wasn't going to tell him that!

That night they slept on board, by the time the yacht 'tied up' it was 3:00 am and Claire was still hanging over the rail.

"Come on, Claire, bed now!"

Reluctantly, she followed him to their cabin, longing for the morning and her first sight of this exciting city.

Chapter 18

The ubiquitous Georgios was on the quayside, a stretch limo nearby.

"Another car, Kostas," Claire remarked.

"Georgios hires them whenever we stop over for a few days. I don't bother keeping cars all over the world. What would be the point?"

The next few days were exciting. Every evening they dined in one exclusive restaurant after another. There was no question of reserving a table. Kostas was in town. He was on the 'A' list and a table was instantly available whenever he chose to appear.

The newspapers sent the photographers on the prowl and pictures of the newlyweds appeared daily. Women's Wear Daily asked if they could interview the bride.

At first, Claire demurred but Kostas encouraged her, saying she would probably enjoy it, at least the first time, he laughed as he reminded her about first times and Claire tried hard to smile appreciatively at what he obviously considered a clever observation.

In fact, she did enjoy the interview. The photographer took great pains to arrange her 'properly' and 'elegantly' on one of the Louis Quinze chairs in the salon.

The reporter was a woman much closer to Claire's age. She wore a smart black trouser suit that she confessed was an Armani when Claire admired it. She immediately decided she would like one very similar.

For her part, the reporter found her subject open and friendly, apparently enjoying her new lifestyle.

"Is it correct", the reporter enquired "that your maiden name was McInnes?"

When Claire nodded, she enquired further about a possible connection with Fiona McInnes, the artist.

"My sister," Claire's response was cool. She really didn't want to talk about Fiona now; this was <u>her</u> interview. The reporter took the hint and moved on to discuss the future itinerary of the extended honeymoon.

"New York, Paris, then to Nice to meet up again with The Pandora."

The reporter scribbled frantically, then took a breath before asking the final and trickiest question.

"Your husband doesn't have the greatest track record in the marriage stakes. Do you think you will be more successful than your predecessors?"

Claire gave a short laugh, playing for time.

Would she? Would she?

"Marriage, any marriage is a gamble, but if people are determined to make it work, then it will."

"And you are determined?"

"That goes without saying," she deliberately made her tone cool and stood up to indicate that the interview was over and that she had other more important things to do. The reporter took the hint and in a few minutes, she and her photographer were on terra firma.

"Satisfied?" the photographer wanted to know.

"I think so, she's nice, but doesn't give a lot away, does she?"

"Would you?" her colleague grinned.

The time in San Francisco was all too short, then they were flying, by private plane of course, to New York. Claire learned that Kostas kept a flat there and she was looking forward to seeing it. She was not disappointed. It was on 5th Avenue, in a prestigious block where a number of 'important people' had first or second homes.

She was surprised at the spaciousness of the rooms and the number of bedrooms, with of course their own en suites.

"Six bedrooms", she exclaimed, "and that's not including the master suite."

If The Pandora was splendidly elegant, this had about an air of decadence about it. Crystal chandeliers; red was the predominant colour and the dining room could seat 20 people with ease.

Kostas was busy.

"Go shopping," he instructed. "Lots of smart clothes. Have a real spend."

Claire was finding spending easier by the day, but the more she bought for some unaccountable reason, the less pleasure it seemed to give her and she was lonely.

She missed Harris and Peter, even Michael and Helen. She had no one to chat over her purchases, no one to gossip with. She hardly saw Kostas. He seemed to be permanently negotiating some deal or another. Frederick hovered, as he was wont to do. When he was not with Kostas, which as it was, was not all that often, he offered instead to be her escort and advisor. She tried, with as good as grace as possible, to turn him down, and he took the hint and hovered less, which in a perverse way annoyed her even more, as she didn't even have him to comment on the ever larger pile of boxes and packages that were delivered almost daily to the flat. Claire now had so many clothes that the maid had to hang things in other dressing rooms. She wore nothing more than once and frequently was surprised to find some of the things that she had acquired.

They dined nightly on the town, had their pictures in everything from the Herald Tribune to the Times and went to the ballet, opera and Broadway.

At least Claire did. It was seldom that Kostas managed to tear himself away from his work.

Her maid became her confidante and was one of the few people who felt sorry for Claire.

She had everything and nothing, she told her maid out of Frederick's hearing. They didn't like him. He was always hovering around as if trying to listen to their private conversations.

The time in New York came to an end. Paris was the next port of call.

Once again, Claire found herself in the luxury of the Lear Jet in the comfort of the leather seats. Frederick poured their drinks and then sat with Kostas as ever deeply involved in business discussions; Claire now beginning to understand a little of the enormity of Kostas' empire, the shipping the hotels and lately the computer industry.

He was, according to Frederick, in one of his less discreet moments making enough of a fortune on software packages to rival Bill Gates. He had become something of an expert and Claire had to admit he was certainly a clever man. They were talking in Greek. At first, Claire had let the sounds wash over her, but every now and again, a word or phrase seemed to jump out at her. She was understanding more and more. Frederick no longer gave her lessons and correctly as it happens, Claire decided that he and Kostas preferred her to be less conversant rather than more.

"Get two," Claire heard.

Two of what? she wondered.

"From Nice to Assos," he continued. "Maybe three."

She was tempted to ask but managed with some difficulty to contain her curiosity. She closed her eyes and after a few moments she heard Frederick say, "You have worn your bride out, my friend. She is asleep."

"She will have more sleep on board," was the somewhat cryptic response. Perhaps she didn't understand correctly. She nearly opened her eyes to ask what they meant.

"Ages?" Kostas asked.

A strange question with no relevance that Claire could see to the previous conversation.

"Six or seven," was Frederick's response.

"Excellent".

Six or seven what? She would have to continue working on her Greek.

She always spoke to the crew in Greek, but they were too polite to correct her, though, so she could never learn from them. She would have to buy a really good grammar and conversation book and get involved in some private study.

She smiled involuntarily. Who would ever have believed she would want to study!

"Your bride smiles in her sleep," Frederick sounded concerned.

"She is dreaming of our lovemaking," Kostas replied with a laugh that sounded rather cruel to Claire.

Finally, she fell asleep and only woke when Frederick tapped her on the shoulder to offer her a tray of lunch.

Chapter 19

Paris was probably the most exciting experience to date in Claire's entire life. She became a total tourist and with Georgios once again on hand to drive her around, she was taken wherever she wanted to go.

Versailles amazed her. She used her imagination to good effect, imagining the court of Marie Antoinette. She was interested to note that the furnishings bore a strong resemblance to the furnishings both in 'their' quarters in The Pandora and the New York flat. In Paris, they stayed in a hotel. Not just any hotel, but one owned by Kostas himself, like the Ritz owned by Mohammed Al Fayed. Kostas used the hotel as his Paris base.

Of course, they had the penthouse with four bedrooms and four bathrooms. Frederick stayed on the floor below and Claire had no idea where Georgios was. He would telephone her at 9:00 am every morning and ask her if she had any use for him. Kostas left at 8:00 am most mornings. She had no idea where he went, or what he did.

When she asked, he just waved his hands vaguely.

"Don't bother yourself, Claire, this is your honeymoon. Enjoy, spend money."

"It's your honeymoon too, Kostas."

He had looked at her strangely as if realising for the first time that it took two to have a honeymoon.

In Paris, though, they did spend several evenings a week together, never staying in, always going somewhere to 'be seen'. Kostas and his bride ate at the Ritz, they were seen in the Casino Royale, Maxims or in Montmartre. Claire remembered the picture her sister Fiona had had drawn in Montmartre as a teenager and how years later the artist was the man she married after her first husband's death.

She tried looking at Paris through Fiona's artistic eyes and wished she too was artistic. She even had her picture drawn but threw it in a rubbish bin. It's not that it was not well executed, it's just that she didn't like the expression on her face. She looked drawn and distant. It made her cross. She was happy here in Paris on her honeymoon.

Georgios drove her to all the major fashion houses. She had become totally engrossed in clothes and the couturiers aware of her spending powers paid her lavish attention.

She bought jewellery, but only costume, even though from Dior or Chanel that was expensive enough. Kostas had made it clear that any real jewellery would be bought by him and on their last evening in Paris, as they ate in Maxims, he handed her a small square box.

"For your patience, Claire. I have been busier than I intended. Forgive me."

Claire was taken aback, Kostas asking her forgiveness. Perhaps her attitude, her just getting on with life, with or without him was appreciated after all. She opened the box and found a stunning gold bracelet set with diamonds and emeralds to match the necklace he had given her before.

"It's beautiful," she breathed, taking it out of its nest and handing it to him, she held out her wrist. He carefully laid it on her delicate looking wrist and fastened it.

She shook her arm and the lights made the jewels flourish. Another brighter flash startled her. She looked up to see three photographers. Their flashlights flashed again. Kostas glared them away and a thought crossed her mind that this could have been prearranged to photograph the opening and receiving of her new bracelet.

Her stomach churned, she felt uncomfortable, almost betrayed. What could she do or say, nothing? She would do nothing.

She picked up her glass and sipped her wine, grappling with thoughts that were at best uncharitable and at worst deeply cynical of his motives.

The bracelet was not a love gift at all, just a chance to have his name in the paper for apparently the most charming of gestures.

Fleetingly, Claire thought of her old life of her friends back on Vancouver Island. Life had some meaning, some purpose then. Now she could see endless years stretching ahead, spending, buying, being generally pampered, serviced by beauticians or hairdressers and as the years went by, spending yet more to try to keep her youthful looks, else Kostas would calmly move on to someone else.

Although she tried to cover her feelings, her subdued demeanour irritated Kostas. Damn it, he'd given her a pretty present, the least she could do was act pleased and happy.

That night, as on other nights, he did not come to her room. She did not know whether to be glad or sorry. Part of her felt piqued, whilst another part of her felt relief that she would not have to play act emotions she frequently didn't feel.

Despite herself, he did turn her on. Sometimes, he would be quite cruel and when she moaned from pain, not pleasure, she could feel his hardness swell. He liked to hurt her and she felt very alone.

Tonight, once she was sure he was not there, she put her light back on and read for a while, one of the sure ways she knew to make her feel soporific.

Later, she heard a door slam and looked in surprise at her bedside clock. It was 3:00 am. She had been asleep. Kostas had obviously been out and had now returned. She lay, hardly daring to breathe in case he came in.

She need not have worried. He went into the adjoining bedroom, which he had adopted as his own.

Chapter 20

She was moored off, as there was no way she could fit on the quayside.

The paintwork gleamed, the brass shone. The crew in their best uniform stood ready to welcome their master and mistress on board.

Claire felt a kind of pleasure and pride as the launch drew up and she was helped in. She felt eyes on her, envying eyes probably, though who knows among them might be someone who knew that to be very rich was not always easy.

Their cabin looked welcoming with flowers on the dressing table and on the coffee table. She had noticed as she walked through their salon that it too had bowls of fruit and flowers everywhere. The crew really did such a good job and she supposed she should give credit where it was due to Frederick, who controlled everything to do with the crew's behaviour and attitude.

That evening, she and Kostas strolled together with Frederick hovering two or three paces behind them, she presumed, protecting his back. It was probably the happiest evening of her marriage, people thronged the promenade – beautiful sun-tanned lithesome young women, gorgeous hunky-looking young men. The lights twinkled, the air was balmy. Kostas, for the first time even, held her hand as they walked. Perhaps, after all, things were going to be alright, perhaps now he was away from the constant work that seemed to keep him so heavily involved all the time, perhaps now, he would devote some time to her, and instead of feeling dread she felt her spirits lift and thought that he was not an unkind man really, perhaps just thoughtless.

They ate dinner out in a restaurant overlooking Nice. The owner, as usual when Kostas arrived anywhere, waved them to the most prestigious table and after an aperitif, they enjoyed a delicious dinner, finishing with petit fois to die for.

The only bugbear was Frederick, but at least tonight he didn't intrude into the conversation, but kept himself to himself, it was almost as if he wasn't there.

Georgios was outside but when Claire demurred, Kostas agreed that it was such a perfect evening that they would walk back to the launch. Once on board the yacht, Kostas insisted on a night cap and poured her a brandy, which he knew she didn't really care for. The taste was, to her mind, horrible, but fortunately he had only poured her a small one and in two to three gulps it was gone.

Kostas smiled broadly and told her to go and make herself beautiful for him. She kissed him on the cheek and walked from the main salon down the corridor to their quarters. Halfway down the corridor, she felt dizzy and leaned against the wall for support. Thoma appeared and was immediately concerned. He helped her down the rest of the corridor through the salon to her cabin.

"Are you alright, Madam?"

Claire was not, but nodded. "Thank you, Thoma, I'm fine."

As soon as he had gone, she struggled to get out of her clothes, but finally gave up, sinking to the bed, she passed out completely.

About half an hour later, Kostas came in, saw that she was not even undressed and rang the bell for Frederick.

"Undress her," he said curtly. "That was too strong. We don't want this bother every night. Half the quantity tomorrow."

Frederick nodded as he pushed her body this way and that.

Soon, she was naked.

"Nightgown," Kostas said tensely.

Frederick went to the dressing room and opened one of the cupboards with total familiarity. Claire would have been devastated if she had known he knew every item of clothing that she had and where they were hung or folded.

He half sat her up and propped her against him whilst he pulled the nightgown over her head. Then lying her down, he pulled the gown down covering the rest of her body.

With one quick movement, he pulled the covers back and unceremoniously dumped her between the silk sheets.

Kostas looked down at her impassively.

"She is pretty," he said almost to himself.

"I suppose so," Frederick said, looking at her as if for the first time. "But not quite to our taste, my friend."

Their easy familiarity would have surprised Claire, who saw the employer/employee role more often displayed.

"Play time," Kostas said, leaving the room without a backward glance.

Claire woke late. Her head felt heavy, her body lethargic. She looked at her watch; it was 9:30 am. Why hadn't anyone woken her? She sat up in bed, noticing the motion of the boat as she did.

The place beside her was undisturbed. Kostas had not slept in their bed. What had happened?

Frantically, she tried to remember the previous evening.

Gradually, her mind cleared. She remembered walking along the corridor and feeling dizzy. Someone helped her. Thoma, Thoma helped her to the cabin. Then her mind went blank. She had no memory of getting undressed. She lay back on the soft pillows, perplexed. Her face suddenly felt hot as she realised that someone had undressed her and put her to bed. Try as she might, she couldn't think who it was. It must have been Kostas, but something in the back of her mind gave her the feeling, the sensation that she had been handled like a sack of potatoes. What was she in, some terrible nightmare? She rang the bell and in seconds, Thoma appeared.

"Orange juice, please and black coffee." He nodded. "Thoma," she began hesitantly, "did you help me last night?"

He looked worried.

"You were sick," he said. "I brought you to your cabin, then I left you."

"Thank you," she said, smiling at him, trying to stop the worried look that he was giving her.

"Orange juice," she repeated.

He nodded and closed the door behind him.

It was 11:00 am before she appeared on the aft deck. Kostas was on the mobile and Frederick had a sheaf of papers in front of him. The sky was blue and the only breeze was that caused by the motion of the boat gliding through the water.

"Ah," said Kostas ending his conversation. "My sleepy bride has finally emerged."

He smiled at her warmly and for a moment she was disconcerted. He seemed unconcerned that she had fallen asleep before he came to bed.

"I don't seem to remember you coming to bed," she said faintly.

He laughed and Frederick joined in, which really annoyed her, but other than the laugh he gave no verbal response.

All day long, Claire felt headachy. She even lay on her bed for an hour in the afternoon. She couldn't remember the last time she had done that, other than the day or two before Lenny was born.

By evening, she was totally recovered. Kostas seemed in particularly good form, full of amusing anecdotes and extremely attentive, gradually, Claire felt herself relax, deciding that she must have been sickening for something which she had managed to throw off.

After dinner at Kostas' request, Frederick put on some dance music and they danced together for quite some time.

For a stocky man, he was surprisingly light on his feet, and she found herself enjoying the evening. Even Frederick seemed more pleasant this evening. She began to feel tired and as if sensing this, Kostas led her gently to a chair.

"Sit down, my dear, we've danced enough."

"But I'm enjoying myself," she began.

He patted her arm and bending once, kissed her lightly on the top of his head.

"A nightcap, I think."

For once, Claire was adamant. She didn't like brandy, and she didn't want a nightcap.

Suddenly, feeling relaxed and sentimental, she wanted Kostas to come to their cabin and make love. She whispered in his ear as she stood up.

He looked pleased, she thought, even a little surprised.

"I'll be along soon," he said sotto voce.

Frederick was at the door so she reached it. He opened it with a flourish.

"Goodnight, Claire".

"Goodnight," she responded, wishing somehow he didn't seem quite so familiar with her.

She had to keep reminding himself that he was a close personal friend of Kostas as well as a mere employee.

The cabin felt surprisingly warm and she opened a window. She found herself stumbling around, so tired that it was an effort to shower.

Finally, she climbed into bed and sank gratefully into its softness. For a few minutes, she struggled to keep her eyes open, but finally sleep overcame her and by the time Kostas appeared with Frederick by his side, she was in a sound sleep.

"That's a much better dosage, Frederick." Kostas spoke quietly. "How do you do it, she didn't have a nightcap?"

"I thought that might happen so I added it to her dessert, the sweetness hides any possible taste."

"Excellent," and with that the two men went through Kostas' dressing room and bathroom to the room that lay beyond where their night-time pleasure awaited them.

Chapter 21

One day led to another.

Claire slept more soundly than she had ever done before. She decided that it must be the motion of the boat. The pillow beside her was dented and Kostas told her how much he enjoyed their lovemaking. Claire was too confused and a little afraid to tell him that she remembered nothing of it.

Once when she woke, she found herself lying in his arms. His face had the look of someone who had recently made love. His body warm, his cheeks flushed. She felt nothing. What was happening to her? Was she going mad? Her body felt untouched. When she looked by the morning light, the bed clothes showed no evidence of lovemaking.

She withdrew into herself, her body heavy, her thinking unclear. She longed for her old friends. She had no one.

Even Thoma scuttled away when he saw her coming as if he was deliberately avoiding her.

Kostas was kind, kinder than she deserved, even Frederick was friendly and courteous.

It was her; she was the problem.

She actually asked Kostas if there was anyone with any medical experience on board.

"Frederick is the nearest we have to a doctor," was the response. "Are you ill?"

She shook her head.

No, she was not ill, but she felt very strange.

In desperation, she consulted Frederick, explaining how in the mornings her head felt heavy, almost as if she had a hangover. At night she was so weary she hardly remembered going to bed. She stopped short of telling him she had no recollection of lovemaking.

Frederick expressed concern.

Probably the motion of the boat and being married. All the lovemaking. She looked at him. There was something in his tone that she couldn't identify, not a sneer, not a scorn, an indefinable something.

"Perhaps, you shouldn't have a brandy after dinner," he offered finally.

"I don't," she replied shortly, thinking perhaps unsurprisingly that he was of no help at all.

"Anyway, I didn't have any brandy last night."

He shrugged his shoulders as if dismissing her as a helpless case.

Frustrated, she turned away. She was on her own. There was no one to help her.

Chapter 22

Several weeks later, they arrived in Greek waters.

It was so enchanting looking at the scenery as they passed island after island, heading for the Ionian Sea and Kostas' home.

The Ionian was the most beautiful place in the world, the lushness of the islands, the colourful fishing villages that she explored when the launch took her ashore.

Her small ever-increasing amount of Greek was useful. She enjoyed talking to the shopkeepers, buying fruit, which she ate whilst she drank coffee on the quayside, watching fishermen unravel their nets and mend them as required. Old women would beat small octopi until they were senseless, tender and as far as Claire was concerned, the last thing she would choose to eat.

She discovered Baklava, light layers of pastry with honey and nuts between the layers.

Not something Kostas' chef turned his hand to. Claire was determined to rectify this.

She was used to the feeling of lethargy that started her every morning and the sleepiness that hit her between the eyes at night. Kostas was still treating her gently as if making allowances for his bride, and she appreciated his kindness.

Things changed suddenly. It was as if a dark cloud hung over The Pandora. The launch was waiting for her one day, moored up to the quayside. They were in Fiskado, which she felt was her most favourite place yet.

The captain's cabin had provided her with an entertaining hour as the Captain himself, a buff man in his early 70s served her with coffee and sat down and talked to her. He told her how 20 years earlier this busy little port had been a sleepy backwater. His was the only restaurant, the yachts would come and go, usually quite small yachts in flotillas. Thirty feet in size and five or six people somehow managing to live on them for a week or two.

He had, he told her, the only shower available on several islands, and they would shower and eat at his quayside restaurant.

"A step off the yacht and they would be at their breakfast table," he told her jovially. "Not like your lovely yacht, Madame Papadofulas."

Claire smiled, thinking it might be quite fun to be on a small yacht with a group of friends.

"But now look at Fiskado. Big yachts, crammed one next to the other, lots of restaurants. Little prissy tables with umbrellas. Looks more like St Tropez."

But he laughed. His generous belly shaking as he did. He still loved Fiskado, she could tell, and she thought it the most picturesque place she had visited in the Ionian.

One of the crew sought her out. His face was filled with anxiety. "I have to take you back, Madam," he said. He spoke in Greek. All the crew did these days, she didn't always understand, but she understood this. What puzzled her was his expression.

"Is everything alright?" He shrugged. "We have to leave." With reluctance, Claire stood up and reached for her purse to pay the bill.

"Next time, Madam, next time."

The captain waved his arms expansively. For a moment, Claire hesitated, then she put out her hand and the gnarled hand that shook hers was dry and firm.

"Goodbye, Madam, until we meet again." She smiled warmly, feeling she had made a friend.

Chapter 23

Back on The Pandora, everything was a bustle. The captain passed her in the corridor, his face flushed; a sure sign that Kostas has been extremely rude to him again.

Claire walked into their salon to find Kostas pacing up and down and Frederick talking in what he obviously thought as a soothing tone, but to Claire it seemed extremely irritating.

"At last, Claire. Where have you been?" Kostas didn't wait for her response. "We are leaving now, straightaway."

"But, Kostas, what is the rush? I was so enjoying Fiskado and I thought the plan was to go to Euphemia tomorrow?"

"Plans change," he answered cryptically.

She heard the sound of the engines and excusing herself, went to their cabin to change out of her shoes, clothes and into a bikini.

She could do with a swim, she decided, picking out a bikini from the drawer. Collecting a towel from her bathroom, she was soon upon deck, just in time to catch a last glimpse of Fiskado as it disappeared behind a curve of cliff.

She smiled, remembering the friendly captain. She would certainly return to Fiskado one day, she decided.

The water of the pool washed over her as she let herself sink below its surface.

When she reappeared, gasping slightly, she heard Kostas laugh.

"My mermaid," he said quite pleasantly, holding a glass aloft.

"Drink?" Claire nodded before sinking again and swimming the length of the small pool under water.

Another surprise. She had found that she loved swimming and spent many happy hours in and out of the pool on sailing days.

As she surfaced again, Frederick held out her towel. She took it a shade ungraciously and wrapped it around her for a moment, to keep out the apparently coolness of the air as The Pandora moved steadily forward.

"Perhaps someone will explain to me why the rush?" She said a shade petulantly. "I was enjoying Fiskado and I was sure you said we were staying here at least three days. Why the change of plan?"

She caught a slight glance between the two men and immediately felt excluded and justifiably (in her book) resentful. She hated the way they shared secrets and she wanted to find out what the secret was.

There was silence while Kostas puffed at his cigar and Frederick shuffled yet more documents, before standing up.

"I have work to do," he said briskly as he walked away.

"I don't feel you trust me, Kostas. Why don't you tell me things you share with Frederick?"

He looked at her impassively. "My dear, you must take me as you find me, for better or worse, remember," his laugh did not amuse her, but she realised that she was not going to learn anything more at this point in time, so she decided to change the subject.

"Tell me", she said, "what the plans are for the next few days."

He brightened immediately. "You are going to see my home, my dear, the place where I grew up, where I made decisions about my future. It is the most beautiful place in the world."

"Tell me about it, Kostas. Tell me about your childhood."

But he would not be drawn.

"Wait and see," he said with an amused smile, enjoying teasing her.

They arrived in the large bay of Euphemia a few hours later. Kostas did not want to go ashore; instead, he decided that they should eat dinner, dance and listen to music, mostly Greek, before turning in around 11:00 pm. Claire was still wide awake.

The lethargy had disappeared; she was awake for many of the night hours with Kostas sonorous breathing beside her.

That night they made love. Tonight, he was unusually gentle, almost as if he was afraid of hurting her in some way.

Afterwards, he turned abruptly away from her and seemed to fall instantly asleep.

Claire tossed and turned and finally in the early hours of the morning, she went quietly out of the cabin and up onto the aft deck. The night sky was clean and the skies so bright that she found herself wondering which star was which.

A slight sound made her turn. It was Danos, the captain, pacing in the shadows. He apologised immediately for disturbing her peace, and she realised that it was the first time she had ever been with him when they were not surrounded by other people.

"I was wondering about the stars," she began.

"They interest you, Madam?"

"I'd like to know a bit more than I do. Actually," she laughed, "I don't know anything about them."

He began to talk to her quietly, pointing out the Milky Way, Orion, The Plough.

Gradually, the sky seemed less mysterious and more exciting.

"How do you know all this?" She could sense his smile in the darkness.

"There are many hours of night when you are at sea," was his reply. "My father was a fisherman. He lived by three things: the sea, the sky and the stars. There was never a time that I can remember that I didn't know something about the stars."

Claire yawned, finally starting to feel tired as the sky lightened.

She held out her hand and impulsively shook the captain by the hand.

"*Efaristo*," she said. "Thank you."

She went back to the cabin and climbed back into bed beside the still sleeping Kostas. Her mind was filled with thoughts of stars and dark skies, and she fell asleep trying to remember the names the captain had told her.

Chapter 24

Next morning, the crew made the launch ready.

"Today, my dear," Kostas told her, "I am taking you to Assos."

Claire was surprised that they were going into the launch then she remembered Kostas telling her of the smallness of the bay.

"Wait until you see Assos. You will understand then."

Claire began to feel quite excited. For Kostas to be so obviously happy at the thought of his home village, it must be very special. She imagined something like Fiskado and her spirits lifted at the thought of all the colours and bustle.

She loved the way these Mediterranean villages were so filled with colour. Each small house choosing a bright blue, deep pink, yellow or white so that as they were, at first glance, massed together with the sunlight full on them indeed a kaleidoscope of colour.

"There is the castle." Claire looked upwards expectantly. She saw a towering cliff, and she could pick out a little of the mediaeval ruins that seem to perch on its very top.

The entrance to the harbour was small, and as they passed by the cliff on their right, the tiny village provided a natural curve to their left. It was much smaller than she had envisaged. A tiny curve of sand and behind small houses jostled for space. The bay was so small that one modest yacht anchored 'out' seemed enough, more would seem crowded. The launch drew up at a tiny jetty and used now to the climbing on and off the launch, Claire stepped nimbly ashore. Kostas seemed pleased with her obvious pleasure. Villagers, knowing that he was arriving, gathered to greet him.

Amongst them was a man of about the same age who embraced Kostas warmly.

"We were at school together. Thaddeus and me."

For the first time, Kostas spoke to her in Greek and she felt proud and happy that she understood.

She solemnly shook Thaddeus by the hand, but he was not content with that, and he embraced her warmly and over her head, said, "The best yet, Kostas."

Claire pulled out of his embrace and laughed up at this almost giant of a man.

"Ah, Nico," she heard Kostas say, warmth in his tone.

A young man, much her own age she surmised, came from within the welcoming group.

"This is Thaddeus's son, my factotum. He deals with everything here, right, Nico?"

Nico nodded and shook Kostas by the hand, looking towards Claire as he did so.

"Hello." Once again, she spoke in Greek as she held out her hand. They shook hands briefly.

"Ouzo," boomed Thaddeus.

Within moments, they were in the tiny square, where Thaddeus' restaurant, one of the two tavernas in the village, was located.

Kostas sat at a table and waved Frederick to a chair. Thaddeus disappeared presumably to collect glasses, Ouzo and water.

"Nico will show you the house," Kostas said expansively.

Claire started to protest, then realised it was useless, so feeling rather left out she left the men sitting in the square and feeling anything but Greek, followed Nico to the other side of the square where two wrought iron gates were set into a high wall.

Pushing one of the gates open, Nico preceded her and closed the gate as she passed through. She gasped in sheer pleasure. A perfectly maintained lawn with flower borders and a pathway overhung with vines presented itself. Nico didn't pause to let her admire it all, but continued up the path and pushed open one of the heavy wooden doors.

The coolness and the lack of light struck her, but within moments, Nico had thrown open some shutters and the dark hall was flooded with light. It was beautiful in its simplicity; a large square hall with a marble floor that gleamed. A few chairs dotted around, no rugs, no curtains and yet it seemed furnished appropriately.

"Would you like me to show you around?" Nico spoke in perfect accent-less English.

Claire was surprised and pleased. It would be good to speak English again as less and less frequently Kostas bothered with English and when he spoke, it was heavily accented. Somehow, hearing an apparently pure English sound made her realise not for the first time that she felt a little homesick. She hadn't answered and he repeated the question.

"I'm sorry," Claire said. "I was surprised to hear you speaking English. It quite threw me for a moment."

He smiled and the smile made his eyes crinkle.

A real smile, Claire thought.

She decided she liked this Nico.

The house was interesting though rather sombre, which she understood more when Nico explained that nothing had been changed since madam (Kostas' mother) had died.

"I understand, but how sad," Claire mused.

"Will you change things, Madam?"

"Oh please, call me Claire, I can't call you Nico if you are going to 'madam' me all the time."

He looked slightly uncomfortable.

"If you are sure, Madam. I mean Claire."

It was their laugh that Kostas heard as he walked up the path.

For a moment, he felt jealous; she didn't laugh like that with him, but then he hadn't felt like laughing for the last few days.

He turned abruptly away from the house and looked back up the path. He could still see Thaddeus drinking Ouzo with his friends. For a moment, Kostas felt a pang of envy. Thaddeus had such an uncluttered untroubled life, whilst he… he put his hand in his pocket and felt the paper. The fax had been a relief, but it was still too close for comfort. It might be wise to keep away from Canada for a while.

He was suddenly furious, furious with that stupid bitch Binny. She had got drunk and started shouting her mouth off about him and things she had heard and seen. This was before she had left The Pandora for the last time.

Fortunately, one of his contacts heard about it and got a message to Kostas. He and Frederick had a quick conference and as always in a crisis, Frederick had the right contacts and made immediate arrangements for Binny to disappear. An investigation was needed in the future as to why she had not been dealt with before The Pandora left Canada.

In the meanwhile, the fax in his pocket said simply, 'the deed is done'. No signature, no details – just the basic facts. Binny would not be indiscreet again.

Kostas felt no pity, the girl had been warned and she had been handsomely paid off, particularly as he hadn't thought much of her anyway. She had been purely a ruse to lure Claire, and to get her aboard The Pandora. He took the paper from his pocket and tore it into small pieces. Then holding his hand high, he let the breeze blow the confetti like pieces up and away.

"Goodbye, Binny," he said softly.

Coming out of the house, Claire saw Kostas his arm raised in a friendly wave to his friends outside the taverna. It must be nice for him to come home. She felt warmed towards him, sensing his feelings of homecoming and feeling perhaps his tenseness of the last few days had been because of this. He turned towards her and saw her happy smile. He was pleased she liked his home and the momentary flash of anger he had felt towards her was forgotten. He held out his hand and she grasped it. Quite deliberately, with Nico only feet away, he kissed her lingeringly. If Claire was surprised, she tried not to show it, but his hard, dry lips forcing her mouth open and his tongue darting in and out made her feel almost physically sick, there was something about him that repulsed her more and more and her guilt was the only reason that she was able to respond.

Nico waiting in the shadow saw lovers. He was surprised at his emotions. He liked Kostas. Kostas had always been good to him, but he felt envy for the first time in his life; envy that this unattractive-looking old man should hold such a pearl of beauty in his arms.

Chapter 25

They moved into the house, where Kostas spent most of his time sitting alone in his mother's bedroom.

Claire quickly found white muslin and Nico's mother made up some floating curtains to cover the windows of 'her' bedroom, which Kostas visited irregularly.

With Nico, Claire visited local markets and found a light cover to put over her bed and a throw to put over a heavy dark chair, the room now considerably lightened became her own, her retreat when she felt confused.

She was cool towards Nico, so much so that Kostas commented and told her she should be kinder to his protégé. Nico was courteous and unsurprisingly polite. But it was as if he wore a mask. He showed no emotion and the flashing smile seemed to be buried deep within him.

In truth, he was in total despair. Kostas and Thaddeus spent so much time together and encouraged Nico to take Claire out and about. Nico knew he was falling in love and he felt defeated for the first time in his life. She was married, not only married but to his father's best friend and to his personal benefactor. The man who had paid for his education, giving him the chance to study away from the village school in Assos instead attending the American International School in Athens, where he had been exposed to another bigger world than Assos would ever be.

Claire was disappointed. Nico had seemed so friendly, now he seemed cool, ever polite, but cold. *What is it about Greek men,* Claire thought despairingly, *that makes them so difficult?*

Kostas was leaving Assos, business called. Ten days had been enough for him, ten days when he had tried successfully to forget Binny and her irritating mischief making which, according to emails he had received, were still causing lurid stories to circulate in ever widening circles. He must get out, be seen to be doing some news-catching business deals, buy up a few companies, anything other than twiddling his fingers in Assos.

"Stay here, my dear. Enjoy the rest of your holiday, I will return in six to eight weeks to collect you."

Claire was delighted. She had quite fallen for Assos, had started to make friends and with her Greek improving daily was happy to remain behind in the idyllic spot without Kostas – ever the unknown quantity.

Before he left, he told Nico that he was responsible for Claire's safety and wellbeing.

"You know what I mean, she should be safe here from prying eyes but you are her guardian." Nico nodded grimly. It would be worse than ever now to be with her all the time, longing to run his fingers down her smooth skin, to brush her with gentle kisses, to walk hand in hand under the stars. He jerked back to reality.

"Of course, Kostas, you know you can depend on me."

Chapter 26

Life changed for Claire. She found herself singing around the house, the shutters were open and sunlight flooded throughout the house. She wanted to climb up to the castle and have a picnic. Nico, silent solemn Nico, these days, agreed to organise a picnic and they planned to go the following day, starting before the sun was too high in the sky.

They left at 9:00 am, Nico carrying their lunch and wine and water easily on his back, leaving his hands free to assist Claire when the occasional scramble was necessary.

When she held out her hand for help, he grasped it and hoisted her over the loose rooks. It was almost as if she had received an electric shock, so strong was the impact that she stood stock still.

"Are you alright?" Nico was concerned; she had gone deadly white, then her face flushed.

Perhaps his 'charge' was overheating. She was not used to this much exertion.

He swung the load off his back opened the haversack and pulled out a rug.

"Sit," he almost commanded. Gratefully, Claire sank to the ground, confused emotions shot through her. Her head was down when Nico held out a glass of water. "Drink, Claire, have a drink." Gratefully, she took the glass, not daring to look up least he read something in her expression that would give her away.

All the years, she had hoped she might fall in love, and now too late, much too late she knew she had met the one man who could fulfil her dreams. He sat down beside her on the rug and put a protective arm round her shoulders.

"Claire, are you alright?"

To his consternation, she started to sob. Deep sobs that came from within, the tough, cool, clear-headed Claire had gone forever, she had lost her heart, her everything for what? For nothing and that is why she wept.

He pulled her towards him and found to his horror that he was kissing her tear strewn face – kissing away the salt tears, with a sigh she leaned into him and looked up into his face. Their eyes locked and held, their expressions serious and still. Then as if on cue, their lips came together and Claire felt happiness and peace, a joy that she had never believed possible. Breathless, she said,

"I thought you didn't like me."

"I love you," he said, looking at her tenderly. "What shall we do?"

"Just be together for now, later we can talk," she replied.

Silently, they gathered up the rug and bottle and Nico slung the haversack easily onto his back. Hand in hand, they continued their walk onwards and upwards, hand holding hand, stopping every now and again to look at each other in a maze of wonderment. There were no kisses; it seemed enough for now at least to be able to look at each other honestly and openly and to feel the warmth emanating from each other's firmly held hand.

Finally, they reached the top and there in the coolness of the archway, the only remaining solid structure to survive, they kissed again. Claire had never known such kisses. They seemed to be saying so many things.

"I love you, I want to touch you tenderly. I want to hold you forever." Nico too was feeling emotions he had never felt before.

A young attractive man, he had never wanted for girlfriends. Had had a brief affair with a married woman. But this, he knew, was different. He had never dreamt that love could be so wonderful, so poignant and so terrible.

She belongs to Kostas, his head kept screaming at him, whilst his heart said: *We will work it out, don't despair*.

They continued their walk, still hand in hand. Nico pointed out an old rusty cannon that had lain rusting in undergrowth having fallen off one of the newly crumbled outer walls.

They looked at Assos, a beautiful dot in a far away bay. They looked out beyond the bay to the breathless beauty of the Ionian and finally, almost reluctantly, they found shade and silently ate their lunch, hardly daring to speak because what lay between them no longer needed words.

The sun started to lower in the sky.

"We have to go," Nico spoke suddenly. They had been lying side by side, their hands touching, just savouring the nearness of each other. She stood watching him as he gathered up their picnic remnants and stowed them away, admiring his strong young body, his strength, his beauty.

Yes, she told herself: *he is beautiful, my beautiful Greek.*

"What are you smiling about?" he asked, looking at her suddenly.

"I was thinking how beautiful you are," she replied unhesitatingly, surprised that she could be so open, he might be embarrassed. Not Nico.

"Then we are two beautiful people" he said, laughter in his voice.

"Two beautiful people," she repeated. "If only we were alone in the world."

"No, Claire, not now, not yet. We shall be serious, but not today, today is the first day, nothing must cast a shadow."

But a shadow was cast and they both knew it. Wrapped in their individual thoughts, they went back the way they had come what seemed to Claire like a lifetime agoy. Through the arch they went, no kiss this time, he held her hand over rocky ground, but apart from that they walked silently and apart, neither wanting to return to the truth of reality.

Chapter 27

Reality was worse than Claire could have imagined, for waiting back at the house was the awful Frederick.

"Ah, Claire, Nico," he added curtly. I wondered what you had been up to.

"I beg your pardon, Frederick, but what business is it of yours?"

She was furious.

How dare he be here to spoil her day?

"Kostas sent me to look after you," he said.

He couldn't add that he had been sent to keep Claire away from news from the world. The papers were making much of the Binny/Kostas connection and Claire could make things difficult if she decided to become involved so Kostas had quite deliberately sent him, not to spy on Claire but to keep her in ignorance.

Of course, Claire was convinced that he was there to spy and immediately she felt guilty about Nico.

Why should she though, she reasoned. They had kissed, nothing more, but she knew that for both of them it was so much more, and so hopeless.

For the next few days, she stayed in the house. Frederick used Kostas' office and seemed busy with faxes and emails. Nico went out fishing with his father. Thaddeus knew his son was troubled but waited for him to talk about it. In the event, Nico did not talk except to say he had a problem.

"A problem shared," Thaddeus began.

"Not this time, Dad."

If Thaddeus was mystified, he didn't show it.

Nico had always been a good boy; perhaps, he had got some girl in trouble.

Ah well, he would talk when he was ready and Thaddeus went back to his fishing.

Despite his despondency, Nico caught some great fish and that evening he wrapped the best one and, using it as an excuse, went to the house.

Usually he let himself in. After all, he was responsible for this house in Kostas' absence, but tonight he couldn't, the mistress of the house was at home now.

He pulled the bell pull and heard the sound echoing around the hall. From somewhere, he heard footsteps. Then lighter ones and a voice, her voice saying,

"It's alright, Frederick. I'll go to the door."

She stood there, her face flushed. She wore a pair of shorts which showed off her long, tanned legs and a brief top which finished just below her breasts.

He held out the fish.

"For your supper, Madam," he said.

"Oh, do call me Claire," she said impatiently, beginning to think she must have dreamt what happened a few days before.

"Sorry," he smiled and as their eyes met, she knew it was still the same for both of them.

"Won't you join us?"

The thought of eating alone with Frederick appalled her and the alternative would be a lonely meal in her room, as she had the last two evenings.

Nico hesitated, sensing it would not be the easiest evening of his life, but Claire's imploring eyes rid him of doubts, and he agreed to stay.

He went out to the kitchen to hand the fish over to the Ioni, a distant cousin who always acted as housekeeper/cook during Kostas' visits.

An hour later, they were enjoying the sword fish preceded by a delicious salad with generous pieces of feta which had been sprinkled with herbs.

Claire was a recent convert to feta and to the amusement of Nico and the raised eyebrows of Frederick, she picked out as many pieces of feta to go with her salad as possible.

The fish melted in her mouth.

"Do you like fishing, Nico?" she asked between mouthfuls.

"Yes, I suppose I do. I've never really thought about it," Nico answered seriously. "It's always been a part of my life, you see. I think my first memory is of going out in my father's old fishing boat. Not like the smart one he has today."

"Thanks to Kostas," Frederick interrupted dryly.

Trust him to say something like that. Claire glared at him, and he lowered his eyes trying to avoid her furious look.

"It wasn't the easiest of dinners, Claire and Nico valiantly trying to avoid each other's eyes in case they gave away their precious secret. Frederick wishing he was with Kostas rather than 'the bitch' as he always thought of her, even referred to her sometimes in these terms to Kostas in one of their more intimate times.

Still, she provided good cover for their 'other' business and if Kostas could get her pregnant so much the better, no one would associate him with their other cargo, as they referred to the boys...

Nico left at 11:00 pm. Claire said a brief goodnight to Frederick and went to her room, carefully locking the door. She had not locked it before Frederick arrived, but something about the way he looked at her sometimes made her feel uncomfortable. Locking the door made her feel safer and on impulse she pushed one of the heavy chairs in front of the door too.

She didn't sleep well. Dreams of her and Nico being chased up the hill to the castle seemed to dominate her night and when she awoke in the morning, all her covers were on the floor. She knew she must have tossed and turned a great deal. Nico arrived after breakfast to suggest he drive her to see the market further along the coast.

An opportunity to get away from the village and Frederick.

Frederick was unconcerned, he knew Kostas had asked Nico to show Claire around and the boy was, as always, doing as he was told. Frederick was grateful that Kostas hadn't delegated him.

As they drove off, they instinctively reached for each other's hand, a quick squeeze and Nico had to let go hurriedly to avoid a heavily-laden donkey whose owner, perched on top of the load, waved at the familiar car and smiled a toothless grin.

"There really are people still like that?" Claire spoke her thoughts aloud.

"Surprisingly many in rural areas," Nico replied. "The cities are about 100 years ahead of some of the farmers, yet there are others who, because they have some money, have moved into more modern agriculture."

After a while, Nico suddenly pulled off the road and drove down the bumpiest track Claire had ever driven on.

"Where are we going?" she shrieked as her body was jolted this way and that.

"My secret place," he said. "Wait and see."

After what seemed an age, but was probably only ten minutes, he stopped the car.

All she could see was undergrowth and hedges. "I don't think much of this," she said laughingly.

For an answer, he got out of the car and came around to her side.

"Follow me," he said mysteriously.

Obediently, she followed and as he ducked and slid through a narrow gap in the hedge, she followed. He held out his hand, "Look, Claire, look."

There, a few yards below, was a small cove with a soft white sandy beach where a few large rocks provided some shady areas.

"Oh, Nico, it's perfect."

"Wait here," he said, disappearing back through the hedge and returning a few moments later with a rug.

"Let's go down," he said, leading the way. He laid the rug carefully on the far side of a huge rock so that they could relax with the sea lapping the sand in front of them and the comfort that the rock provided by way of shade and to lean back on.

"How did you find this?" she wanted to know.

"You have to remember, Claire, this is my home, I know the island like the back of my hand."

"Have you brought anyone here before," she asked, curiosity getting the better of her.

"No," he answered with a smile. "I always knew it would be the place I would bring the love of my life to."

"Oh, Nico, what shall we do?" she began.

He put a finger on her lips. "Shush, Claire, this is our time, let us live it."

She knew what he meant but was almost afraid to let go, all the 'what ifs' entered her mind, what if it all went wrong, what if Kostas found out, what if he broke her heart and what if he didn't really love her? As if reading her mind, he took her face between his hands and started to kiss her.

She closed her eyes, and he kissed the lids, his tongue licked down her nose and then his mouth was on hers. It was not like the first kiss, which had been both tentative and wonderful. This kiss lit a fire where there had been ice.

She clung to him, returning his kisses until gradually they lay down on the rug and made love. It was what she had always dreamed of and had given up all hope of finding. She loved and was loved as never before and afterwards the glow stayed with her, and she knew it always would. Nothing, no one could take this away from her. Nico loved her and she loved him. At that moment nothing else mattered.

Later, they took their clothes off and frolicked in the sea, like small children. Splashing and pushing each other under the cool clear water and making love again, him standing and she entwined around him with the water like velvet wrapped around them. Finally, sadly, and wordlessly, they knew it was time to come back to reality. They dressed and went back to the car and Nico reversed up that terrible track so well that she knew he had done it many times before. *But never with me*, her heart sang, *never with me before*.

Chapter 28

They spent an hour wandering around the market and then reluctantly headed back towards Assos. "You know," said Nico suddenly, "I can never remember dreading returning to Assos before. Home has always seemed a haven and now it will always be the place where I hand you 'back'." Claire was silent. What could she say? She felt the same; the house now seemed like a prison and Frederick, her jailor, and she didn't dare think ahead to Kostas' return.

From then on, Nico would collect her after breakfast and once or twice they returned to the cove, but mostly, he showed her the sights of Cephalonia. They returned to Fiskado and once again Claire sat at 'the Captain's Cabin'. If the captain was surprised to see her with a young Greek instead of her husband, he said nothing, but he said to his wife that night, "You could tell they were in love. I hope Kostas doesn't find out."

"Well, we won't tell him for sure," said his wife, snuggling closer to her warm-hearted husband.

But that was the trouble, they were in love and it showed. Thaddeus realised, prompted by his wife and they tried to warn Nico. "Kostas is my friend," said Thaddeus, "but he has no mercy for people who cross him." Nico was not worried for himself but he was scared for Claire. She however, seemed to have forgotten everything. She tried hard to act coolly and normally in front of Frederick, but it was not all that long before he noticed her glowing looks and happy expression. "Assos obviously suits you," he said caustically one evening. They were dining alone, she and Nico couldn't be together without touching or looking at each other's eyes, devouring as they looked, they didn't dare dine with Frederick. He was no fool. He would have picked up the signals. In fact, he had begun to suspect something so one morning, he watched through his binoculars as they climbed up to the castle yet again. Unsurprised he saw them stop at an interval on the path and embrace. When they finally disappeared from view, he needed little imagination to know what they would in all probability be doing. He licked his lips in anticipation of the revenge, Kostas would take on the girl. He would play her, trap her and probably in the end kill her. It would have to be done very, very carefully though, there were questions, too many questions being asked about Kostas anyway.

Oblivious to their dilemma, the lovers continued unaware and for the next six weeks, their love grew and blossomed. They decided they had no choice but for Claire to leave Kostas and Nico to leave his service. They would manage, after all Claire and he could both work, and they would buy a little cottage on one or another Greek island. Nico seemed to have cousins everywhere and didn't think there would be any difficulties. "I shall become a fisherman like my father," he decided.

"I will open a restaurant and serve your fish," was Claire's response. These were happy times.

Frederick was unwell, *a touch of sun stroke*, he thought. Ioni informed Claire that Frederick would stay in bed in the coolness of his room with the shutters closed. The newspaper was delivered as usual, but for Claire, seeing it for the first time, it was a surprise.

"Yes," Ioni informed her. "It comes every day and Mr Frederick takes it straight to the study." Picking up the paper, Claire looked despairingly at the Greek. She could speak and understand well these days, but reading it was another matter. About to bin the paper, a photograph on the front page caught her attention. She looked more carefully, it looked like Binny. The photo was set in the middle of a complete column of writing and although Claire couldn't understand it, she finally found a word she recognised, 'Binny'. It was Binny.

Taking the paper with her, she left the house and crossed the square to Nico's house. His mother answered the door and unusually, she did not seem particularly pleased to see Claire, even trying to fob her off when she asked to see Nico. Just then he appeared around the side of the house. Thanking his mother, she turned towards him. "Nico, please help me, I can't read this," she held out the paper and pointed to the salient column.

He read: 'The inquiry held yesterday on the death of Miss Binny Brown agreed that her death had been accidental. According to witnesses, she had been very drunk on the night of the 15th, making all sorts of wild accusations about Kostas Papadofulas, which according to sources were completely unfounded; probably the actions of a jealous woman. Foul play was dismissed as the contusions on her body were undoubtedly caused by the buffeting of her body against the rocks near to where she had fallen in. Kostas Papadofulas' representative in court expressed Mr Papadofulas' sorrow at her death; a dear friend of Kostas was how she was described. Mr Papadofulas' sympathy and concern was noted and his offer to pay for her burial was commended."

"But I met her," Claire said. "Kostas paid her off, she was frightened." Suddenly, she was reminded of the morning the girl came to her cabin. "She tried to warn me," Claire continued, "but I didn't want to know."

"I am beginning to realise, how dangerous it is if you stay with him, Claire. We must make some plans."

"I must get the paper back to the house," she interrupted him. "Frederick never leaves the papers where I can find them, now I understand why. He didn't want me to find out about the inquest. I must go, Nico."

She ran back to the house and put the paper on the table in the house where she had found it. There was no reason for him to even know that she had found it. There was no reason for him to even know she had seen it and now understood it. Undecided what to do, she went up their room and sat on the bed. She must leave, leave today, before it was too late. She stood up and went over to the window, perhaps Nico was out there; she would wave and he would come over. Her heart sank as she looked out. The launch from The Pandora was heading towards the quay, she was too late. Kostas was coming home.

Chapter 29

There was the usual bustle on the quay at the approach of The Pandora's launch. It gave Claire an opportunity to talk to Nico. In the crowd, they were just two of many. Frederick, looking from his bedroom window, saw the two of them in deep conversation and smiled as he remembered all the photographs he had taken of the lovers. He would enjoy showing them to Kostas.

Claire moved to the front and the people gave way smilingly, only Thaddeus frowned when he saw her. He hoped Kostas had come to collect her and take her back to The Pandora, once gone, his son would forget her.

As he had these thoughts, he knew he was fooling himself. Nico was in love, and it appeared so was the girl. He sighed as Kostas stepped ashore.

"Ah, Thaddeus, old friend, here as ever to meet me. Claire, Nico. I hope you have looked after her. Nico," he said, clapping the young man on the back.

"Of course, Kostas." Kostas put his cheek against Claire, she felt the clammy skin against her and a tremor went through her.

Kostas mistook it for excitement at seeing him. She looked more beautiful than he remembered.

Being in Assos obviously suited her as much as it suited him. Someone was missing.

"Frederick," he called.

"He's not well, Kostas. He is confined to his room."

For once, Kostas did not stop in the square for his usual Ouzo, but headed straight for the house, dragging Claire by the hand.

She cast pleading eyes at Nico, but he knew it was not the moment to confront Kostas.

He looked back at her, trying to comfort her. He would be there for her, his eyes said.

Be patient, Claire. We shall escape together soon.

She nodded her head slightly as if agreeing with his message and then turning her back on him, she allowed herself to be led 'home'.

Frederick waited. He knew Kostas well enough to know that he would come straight to his bedroom to see how he was. He was already beginning to feel a great deal better, boosted by the thought of his showing the photographs. He had enjoyed being a voyeur as he followed the lovers down that dreadful track to their trysts. There he photographed them hidden from view by the hedge and brush, as they made love on the beach. He had photos of them running naked, hand in hand into the sea.

In all, about 15 photos. The best. Some were boring, just sitting, talking, but some of the lovemaking made up for that. He had quite enjoyed it.

Typically, Kostas walked in without knocking.

"Well, Frederick, unlike you to be sick."

Frederick stood up. "I'm feeling much better now," he said. "In fact, I was planning to come downstairs later, a touch of sunstroke, that's all."

Kostas looked surprised. "You don't sit in the sun. What the hell have you been up to?"

Frederick gave a smile of pure pleasure.

Kostas would enjoy these. He reached for the photographs.

"Keeping an eye on your bride," he said, handing them over.

Kostas sat down and started going through them.

The first, the embrace on the beach, he looked quickly at the next and his face became even more thunderous.

"She will suffer for this," he said finally, "and, so will he."

Frederick was not disappointed.

"What now?" he asked.

"We return to The Pandora immediately," he said as he left the room.

Claire heard the footsteps and knew Kostas was heading to her bedroom. The door opened and Kostas stood smiling at her.

"My dear, I have come to fetch you back to The Pandora."

"But I thought you were staying for a while?" she began.

He held up his hand as if to silence her.

"Business takes us elsewhere, be ready in ten minutes."

He closed the door softly behind him. No slam, no mood, yet within his manner, she detected something that made her feel uncomfortable. She packed hastily. Perhaps even now hoping that once packed, she and Nico could flee.

She came downstairs, Ioni following her with her cases.

Frederick, still pale, stood by Kostas, deep in conversation. As they heard her footsteps, they both looked up.

For a fleeting second, she saw expressions on their faces that looked almost like hatred.

Then in a flash, there were smiles and congratulations that she had packed so quickly.

Had she imagined those unnerving looks?

She couldn't be sure any more.

Outside in the square, one walked on either side of her.

She felt like a prisoner. She looked in vain for Nico. Even Thaddeus was not there to wave his farewells. The square seemed unusually deserted. Could she make a run for it? Would Thaddeus let her shelter there until Nico returned from wherever he was?

As if reading her thoughts, Kostas tightened his grip on her arm. For the first time in her life, she felt frightened. Onto the launch and out to sea, she glanced backwards, no sign of life in the little town where she had found so much happiness.

It was as if it was a ghost town, nothing stirred, even smoke from the stoves seemed lonely, stretching upwards to the sky.

Oh, Nico, her heart sobbed. *How could you let them take me away like this?*

Chapter 30

Nico watched the receding launch with despair, tears poured down his face, and Thaddeus, mortified that he had roped his son to a chain, wept too.

He had to put Kostas' wishes before those of his only, much loved, son. The message had been clear.

"You failed me, Thaddeus, you keep him away from my wife or he will be dead. Do you understand? Dead!"

Thaddeus knew old friendship or not, his son had put his life on the line for Kostas' wife. His own wife sat wide eyed and white faced as she watched the scene enacted before her eyes.

She had warned Nico, she had tried to warn off the girl. Kostas was a good friend, but a bad enemy. What was to become of Nico?

Once on board, Kostas seemed to relax, even attempted to be jovial, kindly, even.

She looked back at the receding Assos, then she saw their special cove, so small and insignificant from the yacht, yet so full of meaning for her, the tears flowed from her eyes and she thought the lump in her throat would choke her.

Kostas observed all this without comment, until finally he said in an ominously quiet voice, "Missing Assos already, my dear, or is it the handsome Nicolas?"

He knew.

How did he know? That was why the sudden departure.

Oh my God, what will become of me? Nico must find me. How can he, where is he?

"Where is Nico? What have you done to him?"

"Nothing yet. His life depends on you, my dear, think about that. Go to your cabin."

It was not a request, it was a command and Claire left the aft deck thankfully, longing to be alone with her thoughts. Frederick followed her.

She gave him a quick glance of pure hatred. He must have been their betrayer.

"Why are you following me?"

"I have my orders," he replied. Once at the cabin, he looked as if he was going to come in. Claire pulled herself together.

"Leave my cabin at once," she said, trying to sound a composure she didn't feel.

"With pleasure," came the response.

"I just need this," and with a quick movement, he took the key from the lock, closed the door and as she gazed thunderstruck at the door, she heard the key turn, she was a prisoner on board The Pandora.

It was only then that she glanced around the familiar space and saw the photographs spread out on the bed. Her first emotion for a split second was a delight, immediately followed by a hatred for Frederick she hadn't known she was capable of. Carefully, she collected the photos together, each one wrenching her heart. They were, had been, such private, such special moments and now they had cheapened what had been so beautiful.

Silently, she tore them into small pieces, not wanting Kostas or Frederick to see them again. Her face flushed as the thought of Frederick pawing over them. Had he seen them?

Brokenly, she sat on the edge of the bed, consoling herself with the thought that they couldn't take away feelings, the feeling that only she and Nico shared.

She went through the torn pieces, seeking one that showed his darling face. Finally, one of the bits revealed a tiny shot of his face. Almost reverently, she held the tiny scraps in her hand. All she had left of him.

She had to hide it somewhere safe. A smirk crossed her face. She walked to her bikini drawer and carefully lifting a tiny seam in a top she never wore, she carefully placed the minute piece of photograph in the slit and sewed it carefully together. She felt better. She had at least accomplished something, now what? She was not going to give Kostas the satisfaction of shouting for the door to be opened. He couldn't keep her locked in for ever, could he? Her thoughts turned to despair again, how was she ever to get back to Nico?

A knock interrupted her reverie.

"Come in," she answered automatically.

She heard the key turn and Thoma entered the cabin carrying a tray covered with a white damask napkin.

"Your lunch, Madam," he said, carefully putting the tray on the coffee table and taking off the napkin to reveal a bowl of soup, a Greek salad and a small basket of fruit.

Claire got up and moved quickly towards the door, but Thoma moved faster. Looking embarrassed, he said, "I'm sorry, Madam, I have my orders," and he was out of the door. The key turned to lock her in again before she could catch her breath.

Despite everything, she was hungry and there was, she reasoned, no point in starving herself to death. That would be far too easy for Kostas.

As she ate, her mind darted about. Nico was uppermost in the thoughts, but she longed for the comfort and support of Harris and Peter, how horrified they would be at her position and how they had tried to warn her. She was kept locked up for two days, then allowed out for 24 hours until they approached Gibraltar for refuelling.

By now, Claire was feeling jittery. Kostas had spoken not one word to her, but when she was locked up again pre-refuelling, his rather gruesome comment had her worried.

"After Gib, my dear Claire, we shall have seven to nine days before we get to New York. We have things to discuss, you and I."

It was a threat, not even particularly a veiled one.

"Just let me go," she begged. "You know I don't love you, I don't want anything. I just want to be free to go back to Nico."

"Ah, Nico," the two words hung in the air and Claire knew it was useless to ask anything. So instead she started to plan what she would do once she arrived in New York. How she would walk out of the flat and out of his life. She had the jewellery she always wore, which she could walk out with and she would fly straight back to Greece. Before that, however, there was much to happen. Had she ever dreamed of it, she would never have been able to be so strong.

They arrived in Gibraltar and again she was locked away until just before they were due to sail.

Surprisingly, it was Kostas who unlocked the door.

"Brush your hair," he commanded. "Put some lipstick on. The paparazzi are buzzing around the ship and seeing you is the only thing that will satisfy them. You will behave, you understand. Smile when I tell you to."

"I can't smile to order," she protested.

"With your arm twisted behind your back you will do as you are told." His tone was so full of menace that once again, she was reminded of how dangerous he was.

He walked ahead of her and, not unexpectedly, Frederick, who had been waiting outside the door, followed closely behind. Once on deck, Kostas held her closely on her right, but unbeknownst to the photographers. They apparently stood closely together. Kostas had her left wrist in his hand and her arm was pushed up her back.

"You're hurting me," she whispered.

"Then smile, or I will hurt you more."

She managed a warm smile and after a number of more flashes, the photographers had what they had come for and were gone. Claire stood rubbing her sore arm.

"Go to your cabin,"

Kostas said curtly.

"Frederick."

Frederick nodded and followed her and as she entered her cabin, the door slammed shut and once again she was locked in.

She sat on the bed, her head in her hands, no tears now. She had shed so many since she left Assos, now she felt empty and alone.

It grew dark. She felt surprisingly hungry. She drank several glasses of water from the bathroom and although she picked up the telephone to order some food, her ringing was never answered.

164

Finally, with nothing else to do, she showered, put on some pyjamas and climbed into bed. She must have drifted off to sleep, for a slight sound woke her, coming from Kostas' dressing room.

Sitting bolt upright, she wondered if he was planning to join her in bed. Her heart sank; that was the end, how could she cope? But she was still his wife and he could demand his rights, she supposed. Though in this day and age she had the right to say no. but she doubted she would be listened to. Every sound of the engine took them nearer to New York and freedom. He couldn't hold her prisoner forever.

The dressing room door opened and Kostas flicked on the light, and she saw he was wearing one of his night shirts, her heart started to thud uncomfortably.

"Get out of bed and come with me," he ordered peremptorily. Knowing it would be useless to say no, she followed wondering what next.

He pushed open the bathroom door and waved her ahead of him, firmly closing the door behind him and locked it, pocketing the key in the small top pocket of his night shirt. Then he opened a door in the wall that she hadn't even known existed. It looked just like the rest of the tiled wall but swung open at his touch. Once again, he indicated that she should precede him. Once again feeling she had no choice, she did so. The scene that met her eyes was one of such horror that she would never be able to erase it from her mind. The room was small and quite dimly lit. A small boy about nine or ten lay huddled on a mattress, around one wrist he had a shackle from which extended a chain fixed to the wall. She tried to scream, but nothing came out, her mouth was dry, she had heard a child, was it this poor little boy with his tear-stained face?

As if reading her mind, Kostas answered the question for her. "This is not the one you heard, and since then this room has been soundproofed so that we don't have to drug you anymore, not that we need to anyway; you are part of it now."

"Never," she said. "How can you? What did you do to the poor little scrap?"

But she knew, of course she knew. But why was she here?

"Sit down," Kostas indicated one of the two directors chairs. "Frederick".

As she sat, Frederick took first one wrist and tied it to her arm of the chair and then the other.

"Tape, I don't want her putting me off."

Tape was placed across her mouth. She watched in horror as Kostas rolled the boy over, then hitching up his shirt, he thrust himself in the child. Never, never, would she forget the scene. It was like something out of Dante's Inferno.

Satisfied, he rose and unbelievably, Frederick took his place. She closed her eyes, vomit in her throat almost choking her. The boy was still.

"Fainted," Kostas enquired unfeelingly.

"Perhaps more?" was the cryptic reply.

Kostas stood in front of her.

"Seen enough, my dear? Now it is your turn. You don't usually turn me on, but tonight it could be different, sweet revenge for your dalliance with my former protégé, fair, I think, don't you?"

He unceremoniously ripped off the tape. She didn't notice the pain of it, she was still reeling at the actions she had seen. He untied her wrists from the chair and instinctively, she rubbed them where the ropes had bound them too tightly.

"Sore?" enquired Kostas, with a grin at Frederick and they both laughed.

"Get up," Kostas' tone took no brooking. She stood helpless, wanting only to return to her cabin.

"Frederick, her pyjamas."

With no finesse, her silk pyjamas were torn from her body.

"Lie down, woman," Kostas indicated a second mattress.

She continued to stand. So, without further ado, he picked her up and flung her down. Her head hit the wall as she fell. She was terrified, more terrified than she believed possible. Kostas rolled her on to her stomach and entered her as he had the boy. She screamed but he took no notice and then she passed out. She came to far too quickly, he was still in her pushing, pushing, hurting, hurting, she heard Kostas laugh and to her horror realised it was now Frederick inside her.

166

Once again, she fainted. She came to as a naked Frederick carried her poor naked body back to the cabin where he threw her onto the bed with a dry laugh.

"Not bad, Madam, but I still prefer boys, but then so do you." And with that he was gone.

Of Kostas, there was no sign.

She wanted to bathe but couldn't move, she knew she was cut and bleeding but felt too weak.

She must have drifted off to sleep for the light was coming through the windows when she next opened her eyes.

Gingerly, she moved and pain hit her. She staggered to the bathroom and turned on the shower. There was blood on her legs, but her face in the mirror looked the same, pale, yes, but no sign of the ravages of the night. After the shower and still feeling very weak, she pulled a bathrobe around her and was just about to leave the bathroom when she felt sick.

Bending over the bowl, the sickness hit her, and as she washed her face and rinsed her mouth, the truth hit her. She was pregnant. She had been sick like this with Lenny. She was pregnant and it was Nico's child. She put her hand on her flat stomach.

Nico, she remembered.

Now she had to fight, now she had to be free, free to bring up this lovechild with its father in a safe place, a place far from Kostas. Her mind was full of plans, and she quickly decided that she would have to develop some acting skills. More importantly, Kostas must not know she was pregnant. He must also think she was completely cowed and helpless and that she would do anything he pleased. She winced at that last thought, no way did she want a repeat of last night, and anyway, she must protect Nico's unborn child.

A light knock at the door, she recognised as Thoma.

"Come in." She heard the key and Thoma came in with a breakfast tray.

"Are you alright, Madam?"

For a moment, she was startled. Was he in on this too?

"I heard you weren't well, Madam and not wanting dinner last night."

She smiled.

"Thank you, Thoma, I'm fine, thank you."

He handed her the key. "Mr Papadofulas said you are to have it," he said.

She took it gratefully then remembered the other exit, the one she never wanted to go through again.

"Do you have a key for that door, Thoma?" she said, indicating Kostas' dressing room.

"I'm sorry, Madam." He looked genuinely sorry, and Claire felt perhaps she had one friend aboard.

Chapter 31

The next few days were difficult for Claire, all her instincts were to shout or scream, but as she had correctly realised, Kostas preferred her cowed and helpless.

At dinner one evening, talking as he mostly did with Frederick as if she wasn't there, he remarked that he almost preferred the 'old Claire', the one with spirit.

"Pity, really, she is rather a bore now, don't you think, Frederick?"

"I've always thought so," replied Frederick with a triumphant glance in Claire's direction, as if challenging her.

But Claire said nothing, just looked down at her plate and concentrated on thoughts of Nico and their child.

"Cargo gone alright?" She heard Kostas ask.

"As per usual," was the reply.

At last, she understood the mysterious references to cargo she had heard before. The boys, God knows how many of them, they were the cargo.

She shivered.

"Cold, my dear?" Kostas wanted to know. She shook her head, not daring to speak unless she blurted out, unless she confronted them with the truths that she now knew.

A few more days, only a few more days and we shall be in New York.

Chapter 32

Georgios was on the quay, the limo, as ever, gleaming. She had never been as happy to step on terra firma and during the drive to the penthouse suite in Kostas' hotel, her spirit lifted by the second.

She still had nightmares about that dreadful night and the small boy but knew it was too late to help him, now she had to fight for her own survival and her child.

It was a relief to arrive. Kostas disappeared to his study, Frederick followed and unusually, Georgios remained by the only exit from the flat, to the lift.

"Why, Georgios, you don't usually stay?" Claire remarked, hoping against hope he wasn't going to make a habit of it.

"Mr Papadofulas asked me to remain on duty, Madam, in case you wanted to go anywhere."

Which translated, thought Claire, *I am still a prisoner*. But New York meant freedom; it was not the prison The Pandora had become. Once in a store, she could dodge Georgios and lose him, hope was not lost. She went to unpack, carefully putting the 'special bikini' top under everything else.

Several days passed. She had been out but Georgios had instructions to take her only to the couture houses. He assiduously waited outside the door.

Once in desperation, she asked a *vendeuse* if there was another exit. A strange look came over her face.

"I'm sorry, Madam, I'm afraid I can't comment."

The couture houses had been 'got at' in some way and she soon discovered that she had been 'ill'.

A particularly chatty *vendeuse* in another house said how glad she was to see madam looking so well after her little illness.

When Claire raised an eyebrow. The *vendeuse* realised she had spoken out of turn and though Claire tried to draw her out, she would not say anymore.

Chapter 33

Claire was still being sick every morning.

Fortunately, Kostas didn't share her room these days so although she tried to be as discreet as possible, she was not listening to every footstep as she had aboard The Pandora.

One morning, she stood upright, wiping her mouth with a towel and reaching for a glass of water in the same movement, when to her horror she saw Kostas reflected in the mirror. She literally jumped and turned to face him.

"Don't creep up on me like that," she said, forgetting for the first time her now humble role.

"Ah, the spirit is back, I see. Come, I have something to show you."

Grabbing her by the wrist, he almost dragged her to his study.

Once there, he handed her a Greek newspaper.

"You know I can't read Greek," she said, barely glancing at it.

"Then I will help you. A former *protégé* of Kostas Papadofulas was found dead two days ago. His body had been beaten so badly that he was almost unrecognisable. It seems his body was then dumped in a small cove that used to be one of his favourite haunts on the island of Cephalonia."

The article continued.

"Nicolas who had been educated in Athens was the son of a local fisherman but had in recent years acted as an agent for Kostas Papadofulas on the island. His funeral was attended by all the people of his village, Assos. Kostas Papadofulas who had arrived in New York only the day before, very much regretted that he and his wife were unable to attend the ceremony."

Kostas thrust the paper at her. Through her tears, she could see a photograph of a teenage Nico, probably the only one his parents had.

"You killed him." She gasped.

"No! My dear Claire, you give me impossible powers, you know very well that neither I nor Frederick left The Pandora before docking in New York. Surely, you haven't forgotten how we so fruitfully passed the time."

"You have taken Nico from me but you can't take his child."

She wished she could have bitten off her tongue. His rage was unimaginable.

"Whore," he spat on her. "You whore. You shall not have his child."

He reached for the bull whip that, on a previous visit to New York, he had so proudly shown her. "A present from an oil baron friend", he had explained, "who also taught me how to use it."

He certainly hadn't forgotten. The lash reached out and curled round her shoulders, the next round her waist.

Despairingly, she ran for the drawer where she knew Kostas kept a loaded pistol.

"Just in case you ever need it," he had said, showing her how to use it. She prayed as she moved that it was still there.

The next lash curled around her wrist and blood was drawn. She pulled open the small drawer and reached for the pistol. In one triumphant movement, she pulled it out, cocked it and fired. It was the sound that greeted Frederick as he stepped off the lift and rushed to the study.

There she stood, pistol in hand. Kostas lay a few feet away.

Kneeling beside him, Frederick felt his neck.

There was no pulse. Kostas was dead.

Without speaking, he removed the bull whip from the clenched fingers and carefully wiped the handle with his handkerchief and replaced the whip in the corner of the room.

Claire dropped the gun and sank to the floor. She was free, the baby was safe.

She became aware that Frederik was on the telephone.

"A murder," he said. "Mr Kostas Papadofulas, I, I have the murderer here. Yes, I will detain her."

173

He put the telephone down.

"You will die for this," he said slowly.

"It was self-defence."

"Really, then why did I see you shoot him in cold blood, standing before you with nothing in his hands?"

Claire had been slow to realise why he had removed the bull whip. Now she knew. He was trying to remove any trace of evidence that could impact on Kostas. He wanted her to be found guilty of murder. For a moment, she didn't care anymore. Nico was dead; what had she to live for? The baby, of course Nico's child. She wanted to agree with him, but what was the point, she could only hope that the police would recognise the truth.

Chapter 34

The murder of Kostas Papadofulas made headline news across the world, the chief suspect already under arrest, being his wife. Fiona McInnes read the news of her sister's arrest with horror.

Peter and Harris read the same news in Canada and decided they must fly to her support immediately. They arrived at the jail at the same time as Fiona, and they quickly became acquainted.

They all knew it couldn't be true, although, said Harris, he probably deserved to die. The three of them met with Claire's lawyers, were singularly unimpressed and hired a top-flight replacement. It was agreed that at the pre-trial Fiona would stand bail and the fact that she was an internationally acclaimed artist might help Claire's cause.

"A respectable background and so on," the lawyer explained. Fiona decided now was not the time to talk of their terrible childhood. Peter and Harris offered to help with bail money.

"It could well be a quarter of a million dollars", the lawyer informed them, "because of Kostas' wealth."

"But Claire doesn't have access to that," Peter interrupted.

"No matter," the lawyer continued.

"It's alright," Fiona spoke slowly. "I will raise the bail money.

They had all been to visit Claire and were shocked by her pallor. She told each of them about Nico, about his death and about the baby.

Much as she loved Peter and Harris, it was Fiona she clung to.

"It's alright, darling, we won't let anything happen to you, I promise."

Chapter 35

With Fiona holding her hand, her newly appointed lawyer gradually drew the whole story from his client. If Bob Chater was a hardened criminal lawyer, he found he could still be shocked by man's inhumanity to man.

Fiona blanched as the saga of the night in the new soundproofed room aboard The Pandora unfolded, and previous 'cargos' that Claire hadn't comprehended were now discussed.

Bob's secretary made frantic notes.

"Check missing boys around these dates," he spoke more curtly than he intended.

Paedophilia horrified him beyond measure.

"Get a search warrant for The Pandora. Organise a meeting with the crew."

"Thoma might be helpful, I think," Claire said thoughtfully.

She explained about meeting in the corridor early on in her marriage and the 'story' about the sick member of crew who turned out not to have been sick.

"I was stupid not to realise there was something horrible going on, I even heard a child crying and believed it when Kostas told me it was only the seagulls."

She bit her lip in frustration and repeated, "How can I have been so stupid?"

Fiona put her arm round her sister. She had not felt as helpless as this since all these years before when she ran away from home after being raped by Mr Lennard, and the awfulness of leaving Claire and her little brother, Stewie, behind.

Both young women were now weeping.

Bob looked from one to the other. He had to pull them together. "Now, come on," he said more heartily than he felt.

"We have a good cause of self-defence. We have the murder of Nico, the murder of, God knows, how many boys; we have your treatment!" he said, looking at Claire.

"No one can deny you had every reason to hate him and we have police evidence of marks on your wrists from handcuffs and marks left by the bull whip."

"The other marks didn't show much. I was wearing a thick sweater."

"Don't worry, we have a lot of good evidence for self-defence. Frederick himself is heavily implicated in the murders of these boys. It's my job to pull it all together, now don't you worry." Claire felt cheered.

The last thing he said was that he hoped the pre-trial date would be within ten days and that because of her pregnancy he would do everything in his power to accumulate all the necessary facts for an early trial.

"We should get your bail fixed and then you can go home."

"Home," she said bleakly.

"Don't worry, darling, I'll get a flat."

Chapter 36

The next ten days passed all too slowly for Claire.

She felt in a daze, surrounded by women from all walks of life, sleeping in a cell, unable to eat much of the unappetising prison food.

The only bright ray was her regular visits from Fiona, Harris and Peter. They had rented a three bedroom flat together and couldn't wait to have Claire safely with them.

Fiona enjoyed her sister's friends and learned so much about Claire that impressed her. Her slightly wild and wacky sister had become a successful career woman before marrying Kostas. She had her own flat in Canada and two stalwart friends. They persuaded her that in the period between the pre-trial and trial, she should return to England with Fiona to stay with her and Paul and their two children.

An important commission was pending for her, another portrait of a member of the Royal Family. Harris and Peter quite fell in love with her and were fascinated by her stories of the King, whom she had painted just before his coronation.

All the chat helped them temporarily bury their fears. Claire had warned them how clever and evil Frederick was. He had been a lawyer in his previous life, and Claire worried how he might be able to change the facts. She was right to be worried.

Chapter 37

Frederick, meanwhile, was aboard The Pandora. He knew it would not be long before a search warrant would reveal things that would corroborate the story he was sure Claire was telling.

Although there was no access for him or anyone to Kostas' bank accounts. Kostas always kept a great deal of cash in the huge safe on The Pandora. It was this money that Frederick now used as he brightly interviewed each member of the crew, carefully leaving Thoma to the last.

To their surprise and delight, Mr Frederick not only gave each of them a more than generous bonus for as he put it 'their loyal service now and in the future', he had also arranged for them to be transferred to a number of different Greek-owned ships in the K P line. Their only instruction was that if they were asked, they were hired only in the past year and had been given a year's contract and that because it was now null and void, they had moved on.

The fact that a number of them had worked for Kostas for up to ten years was to be omitted should they be traced and asked, but Frederick made it clear he did not expect them to be traced.

In other words, they had only briefly worked on The Pandora. They understood, and Frederick's reputation was such that they had little doubt what might happen to them if they talked.

Clutching their small fortunes to themselves, they left The Pandora in twos and threes, using the shadows of darkness, apart, that is, from the captain and Thoma.

"It was sad", Frederick said, "that our 62-year-old Captain chose that night to have a heart attack.

"He had not", Frederick continued, "been well of late."

The post mortem confirmed a heart attack, but as far as Bob Chater was concerned, it was far too convenient, and he asked the district pathologist to search for any possible alternative that could have caused the precipitation of the attack.

Meanwhile, Thoma and Frederick quietly removed the shackles and converted the soundproof room into a music room. Moving hi-fi, CD and other accruements for music into the room. Two easy chairs were placed there, a few pictures fixed to the soundproof walls and finally the panel in the corridor that led the secret way in, the one Thoma had used to take food to the prisoners was sealed, so that it was like all the other panels in the corridor.

Now, the only access through the room was through the main door, i.e. Claire's cabin, Kostas' dressing room, to bathroom, to music room. The alterations were complete.

Thoma had been happy to do this.

Kostas had always been good to him. Although he hadn't approved, who was he to question others predilections?

Frederick finally sat Thoma down in the salon.

"Well, Thoma, you have given good service to The Pandora and Mr Papadofulas and now it is time you had a good life. Where is your home?"

"Corfu."

"Ah, the beautiful Corfu. Well, Thoma, you should go there, buy a house, find a wife, have some children, never go to sea again."

Thoma smiled. "I've heard how generous you've been, but I would need a small fortune never to work again."

"A small fortune is yours, my dear Thoma, it is what the kindly Kostas would have wanted."

He got up and went to the safe and removed an attaché case. "Open it, Thoma."

Thoma's eyes almost popped out of his head when he saw what was in the case. Dollar bills, hundred dollar bills.

"Now, Thoma, all you have to do is forget you were ever on The Pandora." He looked steadily at the bemused seaman. "Do you understand?"

Thoma nodded. "Just one thing, Mr Frederick. What about madam? She has been arrested."

Frederick waved his hands expansively, "A technicality, American law, you know," he nodded vaguely as if to explain the vagaries of a peculiar system.

"She will be alright then?"

"Of course," he replied.

"Now, off you go to Corfu, buy your house, bank the money. Be discreet. We don't want people to know how generous Kostas was, or they'll be bothering madam when she is out of jail."

Thoma nodded. "The Pandora," he said with a wink. "A beautiful ship, I believe, never been on her myself though."

"Excellent." Frederick stood up.

The interview was over, the last nail was put in place in that bitch Claire's coffin.

His timing was perfect.

It was early the next morning that he heard the commotion on the quay.

Looking from the dining room window, he saw three cars; one police and two others.

With a grimace, he unnecessarily straightened his tie and made his way to the quay side. The ship was strangely silent now, only himself and the cook and valet he had brought from the flat.

There were six of them, two uniformed police and four other men, one introduced himself as Bob Chater. He was intrigued to meet Frederick, having heard so much about him.

Bob had to concede that he certainly presented himself well. Certainly, one would prefer him 'on their side' but from Claire's account to date, it seemed he would be the main witness for the prosecution.

Bob had had a quiet word with the police, saying he was particularly interested in a room off the main 'bedroom'. They walked through the ship, no one quite sure why they were there.

Bob and his colleague headed for Claire's cabin, he recognised it straight away from her description. There was her dressing room, leading to her bathroom and there the door

181

leading to Kostas' facilities, he pushed open the door into the dressing room, opening the cupboards in a cursory way.

"Looking for something special?" The voice cool and sardonic was Frederick's.

"Just looking," was the response.

The bathroom. Ah, the tiled wall. Before he could put his hand on the wall, Frederick was by his side again.

"Allow me to show you the music room," he said.

If Bob felt surprised, he didn't show it. Music room, interesting idea. Even he was surprised by what he saw. Two comfortable chairs, soft lamps on small tables. An extravagant music centre on shelving that was totally in keeping.

Clever, thought Bob. *This is very clever*.

"I notice the room is soundproofed," he said idly.

"Ah, yes," Frederick responded as smoothly as ever. "Mr Papadofulas liked to play his music loudly. Not wanting to disturb guests aboard or his wife, if she was sleeping, he thoughtfully had the room soundproofed."

Bob caught his eye and for a moment their eyes locked. Bob Chater knew he was lying and Frederick knew he knew, but he also knew he had been too clever for this American lawyer.

There was a big pause.

"We would like to interview the crew," Bob said as they walked back the way they had come.

"Ah, sadly, the crew has left." Even Bob was startled.

"How do you mean, 'left'? Surely they knew there would be enquiries?"

"Their contracts concluded at the end of the voyage. If you wish to see copies, I have them in the safe." Bob shrugged.

"Yes," he answered curtly, knowing they would be bona fide, if only completed the day before.

Once again, he acknowledged here was a formidable witness for the prosecution, a challenging adversary.

He would have to pull out all the stops.

His assistant already looked tense. There would have to be some very serious work done very quickly, tracking down the crew would be head of the list before the trails grew cold.

Claire was flabbergasted when Bob told her about the crew.

"That's nonsense," she said when Bob explained Frederick had shown him the contracts.

"The crew had been with him for years. He told me so himself and so, for that matter, did Frederick. He will have produced the contracts since Kostas' death. He thinks ahead all the time, I'm sure."

"I'm sure you are right, Claire, but unless we can find any of the crew to substantiate that then Frederick can swear that is the case, if he has a mind to. Now, the good news," he said, determined not to let her get too despondent.

"The pre-trial date is in three days. It is really a formality in many ways. Unless the judge thinks you will skip the country you should get bail."

"I'll be out of here? Oh, thank God."

He hadn't the heart to tell her the case looked very bleak, he was convinced that everything she had told him was the truth but Frederick was undoubtedly going to have a completely different tale to tell.

The pre-trial was ordeal enough. Harris, Peter and Fiona sat together. Claire sat with her attorney and his team. The district attorney went on about the murder and how she should be confined until the trial.

Just when Claire thought she could bear no more, Bob put the case for letting her out on bail.

"She is also pregnant," he concluded. The judge looked startled.

"Who is the father of the child?" Bob looked at Claire and smiled, her eyes were burning with tears. "Nicholas _____."

"I see." The judge asked the two attorneys to join him in his chambers. Claire was shown to an ante room and her supporters joined her moments later.

They all hugged her. Fiona wiped Claire's tears with a handkerchief retrieved from her bag.

In chambers, the judge was discussing how quickly the two attorneys could proceed. "Pregnancy always complicates matter," she knew.

"Mr Jefferson, how soon can the district attorney's office proceed?"

"Your Honour, it is such an open-and-shut case, and we have a witness who not only arrived seconds after the shooting but can also provide us with very interesting details about her past."

"Thank you, Mr Jefferson. That is most helpful. Mr Chater?" Bob Chater was concerned he needed time, he also needed Claire out on bail, but he agreed that with Claire's pregnancy it would be better to proceed as quickly as possible,

"Providing", he stated, "it is not going to damage my client's case."

It was agreed that eight weeks should be sufficient.

"I shall oppose bail," Mr Jefferson said almost as a matter of course.

The judge looked at Bob Chater. "This young widow has been to hell and back," he said. "I think it imperative for her and for the health of her child that there is bail." The judge looked thoughtful. "I shall return to court in half an hour."

Bob went straight to the ante room to join Claire, Fiona and her friends.

"Half an hour," he said. "I am almost certain the judge will grant bail."

It was tense back in the court. Claire thought the judge looked stern. She called the two attorneys to the front.

"I have decided on bail, Mr Jefferson, this woman is neither a danger to herself or others. She will be confined to New York City. Her passport will be held by the court and a bail of a quarter of a million dollars will be required." Lawn Jefferson looked annoyed, but he shrugged his shoulders.

"So be it," he said, "if she can come up with the bail."

The court was silent as the attorneys returned to their tables. Bob looked at Claire and gave a slight nod.

"All rise. Claire Papadofulas, you are charged with the murder of your husband, Kostas Papadofulas. However, bail will be allowed with the payment of a quarter of a million dollars, you will remain in New York and your passport confiscated. Do you understand?" Claire nodded.

"Who will stand bail?"

"Fiona McInnes, sister of the defendant."

"Is she in court?" Fiona stood.

"You understand if your sister breaks the terms of bail you will forfeit this money?"

"My sister will abide by the Court rules." Fiona said firmly, wishing Paul was by her side to give her support. How she missed him and the children.

Chapter 38

They were outside. Despite the fact that they had been allowed to use a side exit, there were still photographers. Claire was protected by Bob as she climbed into his car, followed closely by Fiona, Peter and Harris.

"Lose them," Bob said to the driver. "Then to the flat."

"What flat? I'm not going back there."

"It's alright, darling. I've rented a place for the four of us." Claire looked at her gratefully.

"Oh, Fi, what would I have done without you?" she said.

"Hey, that's what sisters are for, darling, right?"

"Right." She received a tiny smile from Claire.

Claire had never been so thankful to be somewhere so normal. A nice flat with light airy rooms not far from Central Park on the 12th floor. Well away from prying eyes.

There were three double bedrooms. Fiona had given Claire what she thought was the nicest, a twin-bedded room in shades of blue and white, both restful and uncluttered. Harris and Peter had the one double-bedded room, and she had the other twin-bedded room. She was surprised and pleased when Claire asked if she, Fiona, would share her room.

"Part of me wants to be alone, but, Fi, I'd really prefer it if you could be with me, at least at first."

For a day or two anyway, darling," she answered.

She knew she had to return home, but not yet, and she would, of course, be back for the trial. Harris had been given compassionate extended time off by Michael and Peter told his business partner in the salon he would just have to manage without him. They were determined to stay with Claire come what may.

When her friends told her they were staying, Claire shed the happiest tears she had shed for a long time, and Fiona took the opportunity to tell Claire of her own plans. There was a time when the old Claire, the one of their childhood, would have been difficult. But this sister who was becoming daily more precious to her understood at once.

"By the way, Fi, I've been meaning to ask. Does Stewie know?"

"Who is Stewie?"

"Harris and Peter, you sound like a Greek chorus," said Fiona, laughing, and then could have bitten off her tongue, but Claire hadn't seemed to notice, she was still waiting for an answer about Stewie.

"Stewie", she explained, "is our brother. He was in the army, but now he has a small farm in Ireland, a wife, yes, Claire," she said, responding to Claire's questioning look "and, like me, a couple of children. Yes, he does know and I have a letter for you from him. I was keeping it for the right moment."

She opened her bag and, taking it out, handed it to Claire, who tore it open eagerly. It was so long since she had even thought about him. She never had been much of a correspondent. Fiona looking on, hoped Stewart had been tactful, he was always so scornful about her leaving Uncle Len, not knowing all the facts, but blood being thicker than water, she felt sure he would be supportive. She need not have worried.

The letter read, *Dear Claire, Well, you do get yourself into some scrapes, however; knowing you, you will manage to sort this one out too. I run a farm for my father-in-law and he and my wife (Jenny) will take over so that I can come to New York for the trial. Of course, we all know you are innocent of the charges. Fiona has phoned a number of times, and I can't believe what you have been through. Anyway, sis dear, see you in court, as they say, and seriously now, I love you and will be there gunning for you, your brother, Stewart.*

Claire smiled as she passed the letter to her sister.

"It's like hearing from someone I don't know," she said.

"It has been a long time since we've been in touch and so much has happened."

187

Fiona smiled, "Stewie's a good man. His wife is a lovely person. Paul and I have enjoyed some happy times with them in Ireland."

"Tell me about Ireland," said Harris, "I think my family came from there a long time ago."

"I didn't know that," Peter said accusingly.

"Have to keep a few secrets up my sleeve," grinned Harris.

The banter was good for Claire, it temporarily, at least, took her mind off her terrible problems.

As she lay in bed, the scene just before she fired the gun kept flashing into her mind.

She had to defend herself, she had no choice. He would have killed her, and her child, of that she was convinced and that, as Bob Charter told her, was what she had to hang on to.

Chapter 39

Bob Chater was having a difficult time. Using all his ingenuity and knowledge, all his staff were working longer hours than he could ever remember, he was still making little headway.

He met obstacles at every turn and recognised the thorough handiwork of Frederick. He could admire the skill of the man whilst loathing his actions. Bob had no doubt that Claire was telling the truth about Kostas, and now Frederick had covered their tracks so thoroughly that he was frustrated at every turn.

The second post mortem on the captain was no help. His heart was apparently in bad shape, he could have died at any time. There was nothing that pointed to murder, yet Bob knew in his bones that the captain's death had been precipitated. He had one of his assistants working on missing boys from locations at periods when The Pandora was in the vicinity, but that too was proving almost impossible, apart from one or two minor leads.

Bob's chief frustration, though, was the crew; they seemed to have disappeared off the face of the earth. They had managed to finally locate a second engineer, who swore blue he had only worked for Kostas for six months, had never even met Claire, in fact, according to his account, he lived, ate and slept in the engine room! He was of absolutely no use at all.

Of Thoma, the one crew member Claire said could be of real use, there was no sign. He had taken food trays to the boys, she knew that now. He also had expressed concern for her once and she believed deep down he would have helped her if he could. They pulled out all the stops, shipping lines all over the world were contacted, questions asked of seamen in ports that regularly had visiting Greek ships.

It was as if he had never existed. Bob had no one to corroborate Claire's story, and photographs of the 'music room' looked just that, he despaired. At the moment, at least, it was Claire's word against Frederick's.

The time went all too quickly, at least for the defence team. For Claire, the time dragged. Occasionally, Harris and Peter prevailed on her to come out for a meal and wearing a wig and dark glasses, she generally went unrecognised, but just once or twice, she was aware of a buzz of conversation as she entered a restaurant escorted by her two stalwart friends. Fiona had returned to England, though she telephoned every day. Claire depended on the phone calls now and also chatted to Fiona's French husband, Paul and Fiona's son by her first marriage, Baynton and their daughter, Flora. She felt she had a real family and they lifted her spirits, if only temporarily.

Of Harris and Peter, she had no words to express her thanks. They were family and friends, rolled together. They protected, cajoled, bullied, and consoled her, helped her through her blackest moments, comforted her when she had nightmares that made her scream and all the time Nico's child was safe as she felt the baby move now, a tiny flutter like a butterfly's wings.

She lay at night, staring unseeingly at the ceiling, her hands resting on her stomach, reliving the moments, the precious times she and Nico had shared.

Silently, she communicated with his child, how loved it was already, how cared for it would be. She didn't allow herself to think of prison. She was innocent, and justice would see to it that she was freed and that the current ordeal would be over.

Chapter 40

Finally, the day came, Fiona had arrived back, this time with the charming Paul accompanying her.

"If only for a few days," he told Claire with his delightful accent. "Then I must return for the children, you understand?"

"Of course," she nodded. "Thank you for being here."

He did not say it was as much for Fiona as for her sister, he had been concerned at her distress these last weeks and wanted to support her too.

Peter had been allowed into the penthouse to collect some clothes for Claire. He had, of course, chosen the perfect outfit to appear in court. Simple Chanel suits, her favourite Ferragamo shoes. Neat tops so that she could take off a jacket if she was too warm and still appear neat and uncluttered. He washed her hair. She was wearing it a little longer now, almost touching her shoulders. He cut it an inch or so shorter and applied lavish conditioner.

The state of her health whether due to the baby or her state of mind had affected the condition of her hair, and he tut-tutted so much that he made her laugh, which delighted him.

"Excellent," they both agreed, when ready for day one of her court appearances, the trial had begun.

Chapter 41

Claire looked at the judge, their eyes met, not one flicker of emotion crossed the judge's face.

Claire felt her heart sink, had she but known the judge felt sorry for her. She had read enough over the years and pre-trial to have some idea what the man was like, but as any true professional, once in court, any personal feelings that she might have were put to one side.

The district attorney stood. The jury had already been selected and sworn in. Now it was his moment.

"This", he said firmly, "is an open-and-shut case. Murder in the first degree. Claire Papadofulas was found by her husband to have had an affair with his protégé Nicolas Arriatis. When faced with this true accusation, she shot him dead."

Bob Chater was on his feet. "Supposition, not fact," he protested.

"Sustained," the judge acknowledged.

For the next hour, Lawn Jefferson held forth and he came out with facts, all of them correct, but slanted in a way that put Claire in the worst possible light.

They had discovered Lenny, adopted now, and living on Vancouver Island. You would have thought she had abandoned him and after some time, Bob Chater protested that all these things were irrelevant, only to be told it was building up a picture of the character of the accused.

Occasionally, Bob won a point, but the district attorney continued to present a damning case of the money-seeking Claire. He had even found out that Hugo had bought the flat and suggested an affair with the husband of her old school friend as a means to an end.

Once again, Bob was on his feet, "Irrelevant."

"Sustained," said the judge before ending the morning session.

"Claire, why didn't you tell me about your son?"

"I didn't think it had anything to do with the case."

"Everything, Claire. I need to know everything however trivial it seems to you." She nodded.

"I did sleep with Hugo once, but there was no ulterior motive. He originally rented the flat for me, just to be out of the way, we both knew it was a mistake. Lenny, well, they had lost a child. Lenny seemed so happy with them, it was really only a temporary arrangement whilst I found a job, but in the end they asked to adopt him." She shrugged.

"It may sound as if I was abandoning him, but I had never seen him so happy and we, Lenny and I, well," she sounded upset now, thinking of how much she loved her unborn child already, "perhaps I was too young when I had him, but I never really took to him. God, that sounds awful."

She knew what a bad mother she had been.

"Bob, I never hurt him or neglected him, it's just that I never really loved him either."

Bob nodded grimly. It was not as if this had an effect on the murder trial directly, but it showed a side of her nature that the press would make much of and that social services would leap on, whether she lost the case or not, she might have to fight to keep her child.

He sighed.

Claire looked at him, she was worried now.

"It's alright, Claire," he said more cheerfully than he felt. "Nothing we can't handle.

Chapter 42

Thoma was enjoying himself. He had found a small eight bedroom hotel for sale. He had seen how smoothly a yacht like The Pandora could be run. He felt sure he could run this. The couple who owned it were retiring. He bought all the furniture and fittings, all the linen, china and glass. He knew much would have to be replaced to meet his standards and it would need decorating and new kitchen and bathrooms first.

That evening, he went to celebrate at the local taverna with newly made friends. He was generous, but not suspiciously so, he remembered Frederick's warnings. He danced Greek fashion with the other men, a line of them weaving the intricate steps.

When he finally sat down, he noticed, for the first time, the table with the three young English-looking women, one had golden hair that gleamed like the sun. Thoma had had women in his life, but he had not become a sailor for nothing! Now he wanted a wife and in the split second he saw her, he knew she was the one for him!

Meg, Pat and Liz were teachers, coming to the end of their two-week holiday. They had holidayed together for the past few years, finding pleasure in each other's company and exploring new places every summer. With four weeks left of the school holiday, Pat was going back to go camping with her boyfriend. Liz was off to stay with her family in Devon and Meg planned just to relax in her tiny flat overlooking Richmond Park.

Thoma's arrival at their table surprised them all. His English was very limited, but he managed to introduce himself and asked if could buy them an Ouzo. The last was mostly done in sign language but was understood and smilingly accepted.

"Your name?" he looked at Liz.

"Liz."

"Liz," he repeated. He looked at Pat intently.

"Pat," she said.

"That's easy to say," he grinned.

He had saved the golden one for the end.

Now he let himself look at her properly. *Her hair was like spun gold*, he thought. *Her eyes, the colour of a summer sky*.

"You?"

"Meg," she replied, annoyed to find herself flushing under his intense scrutiny.

This is the one I would marry, he vowed silently.

The Ouzo arrived, with the carafe of water.

"Better no water," he said, drinking his swiftly down.

By a mix of laugher, hand signals, English and Greek he discovered they were teachers. Meg taught French and German and spoke more Greek than the other two. She had studied ancient Greek at school, which stimulated her to try her hand at Modern Greek. She could make herself understood in a crisis and all three of them had the usual polite and salient phrases. How much, thank you and so on.

He was pleased that Meg spoke a little Greek.

"I teach you more Greek, you teach me more English," he said, addressing her.

"We leave in two days," she managed in Greek.

Then she burst out laughing at the look on Thoma's face.

"You cannot," he said.

"We have to," they chorused.

Finally, after much difficulty and more laughter, he found that school did not start for four more weeks.

"Then you stay, learn Greek," he said clearly addressing only Meg.

She smiled.

"I can't, Thoma. I have to leave the hotel in two days."

"Then you stay at my hotel," he said, taking the photograph that had advertised the hotel he had bought out of his pocket and handing it to her. She passed it to her friends.

"This is yours?" asked Pat.

"Mine, is mine," he replied proudly. "Tomorrow, meet here 10 o'clock, I show you. Yes?"

The girls decided between them quickly. Why not? He seemed pleasant enough. It would be fun to see his hotel. 10 o'clock they agreed. Here at the taverna.

Chapter 43

Thoma didn't sleep much that night. For one thing, it was his first night in the small flat over the kitchen. It was not bad, but there was so much he wanted to do. Having worked on The Pandora, his standards were high, perhaps too high; he told himself, he could never furnish it like The Pandora. Then, he reminded himself, he had the money, he could.

Once again, Frederick's warning voice sounded in his ear. He would furnish it well, but simply, it would be expensive, but will not look too expensive. Problem solved, he turned over and fell into a dreamless sleep.

Only Meg was at the tavern. Thoma arrived exactly at 10 o'clock to find her sitting alone with a cup of coffee in front of her. He looked around for the others.

"They have gone swimming," Meg explained, demonstrating her words with hand movements.

"Ah," was all the delighted Thoma could manage. He had got this Meg to himself!

Together, they drank coffee.

"You help me with English?"

"If you help me with Greek."

They shook hands on it.

"We go now." Meg stood up and Thoma's face registered surprise. How tall she was, his goddess. He stood and moved over to her, his head came up to her shoulders.

He didn't mind. There was just more of her to love. As for Meg, she looked down at this small, smiling Greek and put her arm through his, somehow she felt that he was her destiny.

Chapter 44

The afternoon session was what everyone had been waiting for. The district attorney's one and only witness.

Frederick sat impassively still in the stand, having taken the oath to tell the whole truth.

Claire grimaced. She knew that the one thing he could not do was to tell the truth.

"Let us go back", Lawn Jefferson began, "to when you first met the defendant. She was Claire Lennard then, was she not?"

To listen to Frederick, you would have thought Claire was just another of Kostas' bimbos, a waitress was how he described her.

The press scribbled frantically. He finally arrived at the last scene in Kostas' life. In great detail and seemingly coping with deep emotion, Frederick explained that he had been out on an errand, had just left the penthouse lift and was walking towards the study when the shot rang out.

"Was there any other exit from the study apart from the door you were approaching?"

"No."

"What was the scene as you opened the door?"

"I heard the shot and ran to the door and flung it open. She," he pointed accusingly at Claire, "she was standing in front of him, the gun in her hand, looking triumphantly down at the wonderful man she had just killed."

"Answer the question, do not add personal observations or comments."

"Sorry, Your Honour."

After a few more questions, it was, "Your witness."

Bob Chater stood up, walked over and looked steadily at Frederick. This man had it within his power to send his client to death row. Somehow, he must find the weakness.

He started gently enough, enquiring about the relationship between Frederick and Kostas.

"Would you describe yourself as a typical employee?" he asked.

"In what sense?" Frederick questioned.

"Would you say you were more like a friend, an associate, than a strictly day-to-day business relationship?"

"Mr Papadofulas was always very good to me." Frederick prevaricated.

"Your Honour," Bob Chater glanced at the judge.

"Answer the questions," she directed.

Once again, Bob Chater pursued the same line from a different angle. "Is it correct that you and Mr Papadofulas had shared interests of a personal nature?"

Clare saw Frederick raise his eyebrows and he looked briefly in her direction. "Mr Papadofulas and I shared many personal interests," he said speaking distinctly

"Good food and wine, enjoying beautiful places, being with beautiful people, and of course, mostly enjoying the cut and thrust of the business that were both a hobby as well as a profession."

"Did these pleasures include the company of young boys?"

"Objection, Your Honour, this is besmirching the character of my witness."

"Sustained."

"Let us then approach this from another angle, Mr Frederick. Did you and Kostas include amongst your many pleasures the shared company of the opposite sex?"

"There was much entertaining on board, much of it including beautiful women."

"Did this lead to any sexual relationships?"

"What he may or may not have done behind closed doors was nothing to do with me."

"You may not feel able to talk about Mr Papadofulas and what happened behind closed doors, but I put it to you that one of your shared pleasures was a sexual relationship with his wife."

For a moment, a brief moment, Frederick looked thunderstruck, then with a voice as cold as ice he answered.

"What you have been told, I can't imagine, my relationship with Mrs P was that of tutor. I helped her with her Greek, and as a companion when Kostas was away and, I thought, friend."

"Your Honour, I must object to this entirely unreasonable, unjustified line of questioning of my witness."

"Mr Chater, I really must ask, where you feel this line of questioning is leading?

"Your Honour, what I am trying to do is to demonstrate to the court that the character of the witness is not all it appears to be."

But, however hard he tried, he had nothing that could be proved, they had been unable to locate one single crew member, and even if they had found someone, there was no surety that anything would be known.

Bob tried to bring evidence about guilt association with certain of Kostas' known dealings. He had sailed close to the wind on many occasions, but as the judge pointed out, they were not there to discuss any possible failings of the deceased.

Claire's face became bleaker and bleaker. Frederick was so clever, so devious. She had learned from Bob that the awful room where she was raped by both Kostas and Frederick after witnessing their awful assault on the boy, was now a music room.

Bob had told her exactly how it looked, indeed even showed her photographs, she could hardly believe it was the same room. How could she expect others to believe it?

The judge called an end to the day's proceedings, reconvening the next morning at 10:30 am. She gave the usual warning to the jury not to discuss the case. Most of them felt it was rather boring at the moment but were looking forward to seeing Claire take the stand.

Chapter 45

Two weeks had passed since Thoma and Mega had first met. They both acknowledged it was love at first sight and a warm companionship had developed. Meg's Greek was improving daily, and Thoma was making a big effort to improve his English.

Liz and Pat had returned to England and Meg had move into the best big double bedroom at the hotel, whilst Thoma stayed dutifully in the flat above the kitchens. They had done lots of shopping, ordering new furniture and fabrics for nearly all the rooms and as each room was decorated, furniture arrived and light loose curtain hung at the windows.

The outside had been painted white with Mediterranean blue shutters and doors. It looked a different place already and Thoma only needed a cook and guests to have a business venture off the ground.

Time was passing all too fast, soon Meg would have to return to England. The thought appealed less and less and she found herself wanting to stay in Corfu with Thoma and help him in his new venture.

He begged her to stay, but she knew she had no option but to return to England to give a term's notice at the Girls School in Putney where she was Head of Languages. They talked long into the night before her flight the following morning. They talked in a mixture of English and Greek now, using their own language when unable to find the right one in the other.

"Marry me, Meg." Meg burst out laughing and, seeing his hurt face, was suitably contrite.

"It's too soon, Thoma."

Then she softened the blow. "I will come back at the end of term. I'll give in my notice as promised, I'll live with you. We can talk about marriage later. Okay?"

It was not as okay as Thoma would have liked but she was giving in her notice, she was coming back and she would live with him.

"By then I shall have done the kitchen and the flat and have done the extension."

This was something they had talked about to make the flat a decent-sized home.

"Then we shall have the winter to plan and advertise, so that next spring we have our first guests."

He was like a child with a new toy, all excitement. She wondered at his seemingly bottomless pot of money, he had been vague when she asked.

"Just lucky," was all he would say.

Thoma saw the headline on his arrival back at the hotel. There had been tears in both their eyes as he and Meg said their goodbyes. They had become very close in the past few weeks. The newspaper headline outside the shop screamed at him. 'Kostas Papadofulas' wife gets life for murder'. The car came to a screeching halt and with the engine still running and fumbling for some money, he picked up the paper, paid for it automatically and walked slowly back to the car reading as he walked. Mrs Claire Papadofulas, it seemed had no defence, her plea of self-defence had been mocked by the district attorney who branded everything she had said was a pack of lies. She had had an affair, cheated on her husband, the man who had surrounded her with everything anyone could have wanted. She was a liar. She had arrived in Canada with her ten-year-old son on a visitor visa. She had dumped the son with friends, not even told her husband that she had a child. She had schemed to find a rich husband, had told her friends that's what she wanted. She had made up wicked stories about Kostas, his treatment of her and some cock and bull story about small boys being the 'cargo'. A pathological liar, he had concluded, with no witness able to corroborate any one thing she had said.

On the other hand, the article continued, Kostas' associate and friend Frederick had given a clear and concise statement of fact. He saw her with the gun in her hand; her fingerprints were still on the gun. Kostas' body lay bleeding on the floor and Frederick had arrived in the room only seconds after the shot. The bull whip she had so poignantly described as being welded against her was, in fact, still propped in a corner of the room and she had only vague marks on her body, she said, because her thick sweater protected her.

One small mark on her wrist was all she had to show the police and that did not prove that she had been hit with a bull whip. The jury, Thoma continued to read in horror, were unanimous in their verdict and the pregnant Madame Papadofulas was sent to prison for life.

Thoma was trembling, he felt suddenly dirty. Frederick had tricked him, bribed him, his hotel and all that was in it was bought with dirty money. He had to do something to help madam. Poor thing, he knew a thing or two about the boys. Frederick said that he would be accused as being a party to murder if he spoke out. Well, even if it put him away, how could he live, knowing that Frederick had lied and lied so that Claire, who he made no secret of hating, would be a prisoner for life?

As Meg walked into her flat in Richmond, the telephone was ringing, she smiled. She felt sure she knew who it was. She picked up the telephone.

"Hello, Thoma," she said before he had even said a word.

For the next few minutes, she couldn't understand a word he said. He was speaking so fast in a mix of Greek and English.

Finally, she prevailed upon him to slow down, and gradually, she understood what he was saying. He worked for Kostas. Claire was innocent. He must help. His English was bad. She must telephone America. He must go there. She must come to help. When could she speak to her lawyer? When would Claire be freed?

"Thoma, I understand," she said. "I will try to get hold of the lawyer, I will telephone you when I have."

"Oh, I love you, my Meg."

"I love you too, Thoma," she said, surprising herself.

She wondered what his part in the whole saga was, but she could not believe he would hurt anyone.

With a sigh, she unpacked, feeling she must have some semblance of normality before she started phoning the States and anyway, with the time difference there was no point in phoning yet.

After she had put away all her things, she sat down to read the newspaper to find out what she could, if only the name of a lawyer to contact. To her surprise, she discovered that Claire's sister was Fiona McInnes, the artist. Perhaps that would be the easiest point of contact.

She rang directory enquiries. To her surprise, the number was not ex-directory. A man answered, he sounded French. She had some vague memory of reading about Fiona McInnes after she had painted the King's portrait, she had read she was married to a French man and yes it was all coming back, it was a second marriage, she vaguely remembered. Anyway, she had the correct number.

"May I speak with Fiona McInnes?" she enquired.

"I'm afraid my wife is unable to come to the telephone. Is that a member of the press?"

"Oh no, absolutely not. It's just that I've just come back from Corfu. There is a man, a man I know well. He says he can help, his name is Thoma, and he was a…" she didn't get any further. The phone banged as if dropped, she heard him call: "Fi, Fi darling, a witness, for Claire, come to the phone, quickly."

A moment or two later, a breathless voice answered.

"Fiona McInnes here. You can help my sister?"

No pre-ambles, no wasted time, straight to the point. There was, thought Fiona, no time for niceties. Meg took her cue, introduced herself briefly and then explained how Thoma, an ex-crew member of The Pandora wanted to help Claire.

"About time," Fiona spoke, bitterly remembering her sister's face when the judge announced a life sentence for first-degree murder. Meg felt she had to put the record straight.

"Thoma telephoned me only minutes ago. He had not heard anything until he saw the paper in Corfu today."

"I'm sorry," Fiona said. "You must understand how I feel, the lawyer advertised widely for crew members to come forward and not one did."

"Well, I'm sure Thoma would have, if he'd known. Now what should he do?"

"Leave it to me," was the reply. "Give me your name and telephone number and his full name and telephone number and address."

"He won't be in trouble, will he?" Meg suddenly worried.

"All we need is some corroborative evidence to give us grounds for an appeal."

"I'm sure he'll do anything."

"Good and thank you, Meg, for telephoning. I'll be back in touch with you," and she was gone.

Meg sat down feeling weak at the knees, wondering what she had got herself caught in.

Fiona, without glancing at the clock, put an immediate call through to Bob's personal number. Bob groaned as he reached for the phone, nothing could be this urgent, he thought, glanced at the bedside clock, 2:48 am.

"Yes, Bob Chater."

"Bob, its Fiona, I've found Thoma."

Instantly alert, Bob sat bolt upright in bed and reached for the pad and pen he always kept on his side table.

"Give me the details."

As Fiona passed on the details, only moments before given to her by Meg, she felt an enormous sense that after all things were going to work out.

"Can we organise an appeal now?" she wanted to know.

"Steady, Fiona, we have to move gently on this, we mustn't frighten him off, I'll fly out personally today."

Thinking as he spoke, before Frederick gets to him. Had he but known there was nothing further from Frederick's thoughts, he was comfortably ensconced in the penthouse flat, was going to wind Kostas' affairs up and find himself a house or two in faraway places with the money that he acquired from the many cash filled safes that Kostas had left in strategic places around the world and to which he, Frederick, had sole access.

Chapter 46

The plane landed in Corfu, and Bob collected his luggage from the overhead compartment. He always believed in travelling light and was one of the first passengers outside seeking a taxi. He handed the address to the driver and sat back to admire Corfu.

The meeting with Thoma was not easy. Firstly, Thoma's much improved English seemed to have nearly deserted him. Secondly, when he did speak English, Bob could barely comprehend him. He understood enough though to make Claire's story about young boys seem true.

Finally, he arranged to meet Thoma again the next morning at 9:00 am and he said he would bring with him someone who spoke equally good Greek as English.

Thoma was obviously relieved. Bob decided not to issue a warning about safety, though he knew that once Thoma was engaged as a key witness, his life would be on the line and he would need protection. Frederick had too much to lose.

The next morning at 9:00 am, he was once more at Thoma's now smart looking hotel, this time accompanied by a Greek lawyer he had managed to track down through his New York contacts. There had been many telephone calls between Corfu and New York since his arrival. Bob also called Fiona to at least say he had found Thoma and that the portents looked encouraging.

Thoma was waiting for them and pleased to see a fellow countryman. He reverted entirely to Greek, which was then immediately translated for Bob's benefit. He blessed the day he had learned shorthand, for he was able to take down verbatim every word that Thoma spoke.

What emerged was as grisly a tale as Claire had indicated. Though Thoma confirmed that in the ten years that he had spent on The Pandora, to his knowledge there had been at least 15 boys brought on board as "'cargo' (that word again).

Claire had explained how she had first heard it when she was in court.

"But," Thoma continued, "I was only allowed in that corridor in the last three years.

"Are you saying", his Greek lawyer said, "that in the last three years there have been at least 15 boys?"

Thoma nodded unhappily. "What could I do?" he asked. "I did my best, I took them food and I bathed them."

There was silence.

"What did he say?" Bob demanded. The lawyer translated.

"My God," Bob swore as he wrote, "then how many others?" It was a rhetorical question.

Perhaps only Frederick knew the answer.

"Ask him about the room, he must describe it."

Thoma described it as Claire had. He even added that the soundproofing was done because madam thought she heard a child.

"For a while," he continued, "they, Mr Frederick, drugged her at dinner, once they gave her too much and I found her in the corridor and took her to her cabin."

"What happened to the boys?" Bob asked.

"Usually they died, sometimes not, then they were given big money, but only if Kostas knew they had enjoyed it. Not many, one or two, I think.

"Stephen, one of the crew, was friends with Frederick. He told me that he and Frederick would tie the weights from the gym around them and then they would throw them overboard."

Both lawyers were silent now, their imagination too vivid for their own comfort.

"You will come to New York, Thoma, tell this in court?"

For a moment, Thoma looked frightened. Then he sat up.

"It will help, Madam Claire?"

"It will free her."

"Then I come," he said reverting to English.

That night, Bob slept in the hotel. He wasn't going to let Thoma out of his sight. They talked about a safe place for him to live until the appeal. Suddenly, Thoma smiled. "England," he beamed. "My Meg." He showed the address that Meg had written for him.

"Excellent." Bob said out loud. Secretly delighted, Frederick would never think of tracking a Greek sailor to England.

Chapter 47

Thoma arrived in England and was escorted by the police through the biggest airport he had ever imagined. He wondered how people ever knew which way to go.

Outside, he was shown into a plain black car and his escort came with him as they drove to Richmond. "Always stay with someone," he was warned. "If you feel in any way threatened, you must ring this number. You may not think so, but there will be someone keeping an eye on you at all times."

The plain clothed policeman walked him up the stairs to the first floor flat that was Meg's home. He heard a sound from the inside when he rang the bell and there was his Meg again, her golden hair more lovely than he had remembered, and her smile so warm, so welcoming. "Thoma, well, I didn't expect you to see my home quite so soon." He didn't completely understand, but he liked the tonality of what she said. "I'm here," he said simply.

Bob Chater had telephoned Meg earlier and he had assured her that Thoma would be safe in England. "Frederick has no idea that Thoma has any British contacts, but anyway there will be someone on duty, near the flat at all times, and when he comes to New York for the appeal, we shall make sure he is protected."

"I shall come too," she responded.

Chapter 48

Frederick's agent arrived in Corfu one week after Thoma had left, one day after the date of the appeal had been announced. Thoma had used his last few hours on the island wisely, now no one had ever heard of him, they scratched their heads listening to descriptions of the 5'6" seaman, who might have bought himself a property.

They went to estate agents to check on recent sales, but drew a blank as the agents politely but firmly told them, they could not discuss client's business, even for a bribe. Thoma had come from Corfu, and no one was going to betray a fellow Corfusion. The daughter and son-in-law of the local tavern had moved into the hotel and were continuing the improvements as handed down by Thoma. They were the owners, they assured the snooping agent. Finally, after ten days, the agent contacted Frederick. "He's not here. He's never been here."

"If you can't find him, I don't have to worry." Frederick realised there was no one who would dare come forward; it would lead to their death.

Chapter 49

The day finally dawned. Claire came into court once again, although five months pregnant, she looked frail. "She's lost so much weight," Peter and Harris muttered together. Her shoulders were drooped, she looked defeated. Then, as if compelled, she looked up. There in the galley she saw Fiona and Paul and Stewie, her brother. She hadn't seen him for so long and he came as he said he would, the same for Peter and Harris. Below, to her surprise, she saw Ellie and Hugo and, sitting between them, a bright-looking Lenny. He saw her look at him, and he gave a grin and a thumbs up sign. Suddenly, she felt lighter, her shoulders straightened, all these dear people had come to support her yet again with the addition of Ellie and Hugo, who she had refused point blank to drag in last time, last time when she thought the truth would win. She had no idea why Ellie and Hugo were here and why they had brought Lenny, but she felt a ray, a small ray of hope. "There must always be hope," Bob had said last night, when he briefed her on what to expect in court the following day. The judge entered the court and everyone stood. Claire clutched at the desk, suddenly feeling faint, but she pulled herself together, she had just seen Frederick and his look of venom in her direction, somehow gave her the strength she needed.

"Your Honour," Bob addressed the judge. "As you know there is evidence that was not available when this case was last in court. I should like now to bring my first witness."

To Claire's surprise, Ellie was called to the stand and after she had given her name and had been sworn in, Bob asked her how long she had known the accused. "Claire and I became best friends at school in Edinburgh when we were seven," she explained. "Then my parents made the decision to move to Canada and so until she arrived at my house in Canada, I had not seen her since we were about 12. But," she continued, "We had always exchanged Christmas cards and had kept each other up to date."

You had, Claire thought guiltily, *my cards were hit and miss*.

"So, you would describe Claire as a good friend?"

"Yes."

"When she arrived unannounced were you surprised?"

"I suppose I was a little," Ellie answered. "But I had always written on every card that I hoped she would visit, it was an open invitation."

"She told you, I believe, that she was a widow and this in fact was a lie."

Frederick's face was a study of triumph noted Claire unhappily daring to look at him again.

"It was a lie, yes, but later when we adopted our son Lenny, he told us about his unhappy time at home because in part his father hit his mother and the last time, the worst time was when she told him they were going to leave home and go to Canada."

"So, would you say the lie was justified?"

"No lie can be justified, but explainable and as it happened, Lenny's birth father died not all that long after anyway."

"One final question, my client has been accused of abandoning her son."

"Objection, Your Honour," the district attorney had had enough.

"Mr Chater, is this line of questioning relevant?"

"It is, Your Honour, in that my client's character has been called into disrepute, I wish to present facts to correct that misconception."

The judge nodded. "Proceed."

"Claire left Lenny with us whilst she found a job, he started school and made friends and seemed happy, so the arrangements continued with Claire visiting every weekend." A shadow crossed Ellie's face, and Claire knew what was coming next. "We had recently lost a child, my husband and I were unable to have further children. Somehow, Lenny being there seemed to help and as time went by we began to love him dearly. Claire was, by now, very busy with her work until very late at night, not really perhaps the most suitable arrangement when you have a child. Anyway, we asked her finally if she would consider letting us adopt Lenny, and I believe, after much soul searching she allowed us to adopt him." "Thank you, Mrs Howard. That will be all."

The district attorney waved his hand. "No questions," he said briefly.

Claire watched as Ellie returned to her seat and sat next to Lenny, who leaned over and kissed her cheek. *He never did that to me*, Claire thought ruefully. As if as a reminder, Nico's child gently kicked. She put her hand on her new rounded stomach and sent the baby messages of love.

The morning session was ended. The afternoon session would begin at 2 pm. For Claire, for her family and friends it was an agonising wait. For Thoma, it was nerve-wracking not knowing quite what court would be like, though Meg and Bob had explained. His English, when he kept calm was now very good, the weeks of living with Meg, her patient teaching and his longing to learn had all contributed. Despite that, Bob had a Greek interpreter on hand in case of difficulties. Ignatius Frederick, how he hated his first name, which is why he had been Mr Frederick to the minions and Frederick to his colleagues. He was unconcerned. So, they showed in court this morning that she hadn't abandoned her son, still there were those that would think having him adopted was akin to abandonment. He was unworried. If that was the strength of appeal he had nothing to worry about. A small frown furrowed his brow. That Bob Chater seemed very positive today. The district attorney would not be drawn, he said it had been an open–and-shut case as far as he was concerned and remained so.

Chapter 50

Finally, the afternoon session began. Thoma Lukas was called. Thoma strode in purposefully, determined to show Mr Frederick and anyone else that he was not afraid. He sat after giving his name and the oath and looked around for Meg. There she was, sitting next to a nice-looking lady, who must be madam's sister. He saw Frederick and received such a malevolent look that for a moment he almost lost his nerve. Once more, he glanced up, and Meg gave a little nod as if to say you can do it Thoma, and he could for her and for Miss Claire. He had told Meg everything, he had made her cry, but she had to know what he had been a part of, the whole horror. He was glad he had told her, because in a way the telling helped a little, for every time he told it he avenged the deaths in some small way and this time the telling would help them to understand why Miss Claire had to shoot.

The questioning was intense. There were many tears in court as the ghastly saga unfolded. Even the judge, according to press reports the following day was seen to wipe her eyes. 'The room' and the change wrought in it to turn it from a prison cell to a music room, which had been Frederick's name for it was made very clear. He was shown pictures of the changed room and explained how it had been, which totally corroborated Claire's original statement. More and more of Frederick's evidence was found to be lies but also to hear at last a witness who had seen the children, had taken their food, had even tried in the smallest way to help. Finally, with the tears streaming down his face, Thoma was allowed a break before facing the district attorney's questioning. The judge asked to meet the defence and district Attorney in her rooms.

"Let us be frank," she began. "The person who should be in prison is Ignatius Frederick. I have a mind to overturn the jury verdict. It is, in my opinion, no longer a safe verdict."

She looked expectantly from one to another of her colleagues. Bob Chater was grinning most unprofessionally.

He had seldom felt so delighted about a case. Lawn Jefferson looked slightly tense, but nodded his head in agreement.

"We shall detain Mr Frederick with a view to further enquiries by the district attorney's office with references to a number of alleged offences including kidnap, paedophilia and rape. What a man," she exploded.

Then pulling herself together, "Right, gentlemen, I will see you in court."

Bob Chater had no way of knowing what Claire would face a few months or a year or two. He dare not hope for more, yet there were precedents set that could let her walk free!

The afternoon session started. You could hear a pin drop as everyone settled back to hear what the judge would say.

"Mr Chater," she began and then repeated what she had said earlier in her chambers. Claire heard the words 'unsafe verdict'.

What did it mean? Had this changed anything? Fiona held Paul's hand so tightly that he winced. Harris and Peter held hands too. Lenny lent forward trying to understand what was happening. Frederick sat bolt upright his face impassive.

"Therefore," continued the judge, "the charge has been reduced to manslaughter. A period of ten weeks to be served in prison. However, as that time has already been served, your client, Mr Chater," she paused and looked at Claire, "your client may leave the court today as a free woman."

Claire's knuckles were white as she clutched the front of the dock. She heard the words, but a ringing in her ears and a blackness overcame her.

She did not hear the judge's final words.

"Mr Ignatius Frederick will, however, be detained pending further enquiries by the district attorney's office."

The warden was giving her water – people were cheering – she saw Frederick being led away by wardens. Was she, had she heard correctly, was she free? Everyone crowded round, Harris and Peter hugged her. Fiona and Paul, then slowly and rather shyly Lenny approached. For the first time, Claire opened her arms to him and they hugged.

"Thank you for being here, Lenny." He smiled, returned her hug and stood back.

They were having dinner, Bob and his wife, Claire, Fiona and Paul, Stewie, Harris and Peter, Ellie, Hugo and Lenny, and only Thoma and Meg had declined. Thoma wanted to get away from the big city and he was going to London briefly for Meg to pack and they were returning to Corfu. The school had agreed to release her early. Thoma and Claire had had a private meeting earlier when she thanked him for giving her her life back.

"I should have come before, but I didn't know," he began.

"You came," she said gently. "It was you who saved me from a lifetime in prison. Be happy with your Meg."

He beamed. "Come and see us in Corfu."

"One day perhaps," she answered, wondering where on earth she was going to live.

Chapter 51

It was Stewart who came up with the solution. He and Fiona had wondered where Claire would go.

"The Cottage," he said suddenly. "The Cottage she could stay in, the one we had when we were first married."

"What a perfect idea."

"When shall we tell her?"

"How about now?"

"After dinner," Fiona suggested.

"After dinner it shall be," Stewart said happily. "It will be good to have her close by and the children will love having a new baby cousin!"

Ellie, Hugo and Lenny said their goodbyes as they were flying back to Vancouver Island first thing the next morning. "Come and stay with us anytime," Ellie said. Claire laughed. "That's why I came in the first place, because you kept asking me to."

"What a good job you did, Claire," Hugo said. "You shared your son with us."

Lenny didn't hug her again, but held out his hand. It was strange; she didn't feel like his mother now, any more than she ever had, but she felt something like love towards him. Nico had taught her to love. They smiled into each other's eyes and for the first time, Lenny felt the warmth of love emanating from her, and it somehow heeled a sadness he had not known he felt.

It was just Harris, Peter, Fiona, Paul, Stewart and Claire.

"Now what?" said Claire. There was a busy silence. Harris broke it.

"Claire, we want you to live with us. We want to take care of you and your baby. We'll be its fathers."

For a moment, Claire wanted to scream: "Nico, Nico is my baby's father," but she knew their offer was made with only her best interests and love, so she swallowed hard and reached over and squeezed her two dearest friends by the hand.

"I have a cottage," Steward began.

"Where?" Claire wanted to know.

"In Ireland, on the farm. It's a lovely cottage."

Paul spoke for the first time for a while. "We've been there several times with the children."

"How long can I stay there?" Claire wondered aloud.

"Forever," Stewart said firmly. "Or as long as you want."

"Is there room for us?" Harris asked in the silence that followed.

"There has to be, or I'm not going," Claire said, laughing.

"There is, there is," Stewart repeated.

"Then Ireland it is."

Four months later, on a lovely spring afternoon, Nico's daughter was born in the cottage on the farm.

Claire lay contently in bed with her daughter, her daughter whose hair was the colour of Nico's and who, she convinced herself, looked so much like the man she would always hold dear.

"What will you call her?" Peter said, looking at his flushed and beautiful friend.

"Probably hasn't decided yet," Harris said, coming into the room with a tray of tea for them. They could settle down and be family the midwife had left.

"I have decided." Claire answered. "Bob Chater said once when I was particularly downcast in prison 'hold on Claire, there is always hope'. My baby moved then and I knew she was a little girl, and her name would be Hope."

"Hope," her friends repeated.

"Yes, Hope Nichola."